Master Class

Also by David Pownall

Novels
AFRICAN HORSE
THE RAINING TREE WAR
GOD PERKINS
MY ORGANIC UNCLE *and other stories*
LIGHT ON A HONEYCOMB
BELOVED LATITUDES

Plays
MUSIC TO MURDER BY
THE DREAM OF CHIEF CRAZY HORSE
MOTOCAR *and* RICHARD III PART TWO
AN AUDIENCE CALLED EDOUARD

Poetry
ANOTHER COUNTRY
(*Peterloo*)

Non-fiction
BETWEEN RIBBLE AND LUNE

Master Class

David Pownall

faber and faber
LONDON·BOSTON

First published in 1983
by Faber and Faber Limited
3 Queen Square London WC1N 3AU
Filmset by Wilmaset Birkenhead Merseyside
Printed in Great Britain by
Redwood Burn Ltd
Trowbridge Wiltshire
All rights reserved

All rights whatsoever in this play are strictly reserved
and applications to perform it, etc., must be made
in advance, before rehearsals begin, to
John Johnson, Clerkenwell House, 45–47 Clerkenwell Green,
London EC1R 0HT

British Library Cataloguing in Publication Data

Pownall, David
Master class.
I. Title
822′.914   PR6066.0/
ISBN 0–571–13230–8

Characters

ZHDANOV
PROKOFIEV
SHOSTAKOVICH
STALIN

Master Class opened at the Haymarket Theatre, Leicester, on 27 January 1983. The cast was as follows:

ZHDANOV	Jonathan Adams
PROKOFIEV	Peter Kelly
SHOSTAKOVICH	David Bamber
STALIN	Timothy West

Directed by Justin Greene
Designed by Martin Johns
Composer and Musical Director, John White

The production transferred to the Old Vic Theatre, London, with the same cast, on 18 January 1984.

ACT ONE

A richly decorated reception room in the old Kremlin with a grand piano. A washroom and toilet stand adjacent right. The walls of both rooms are open. The entrance to the sitting room is from upstage. The door adjoining it with the washroom is from the right.

Lights up on ZHDANOV *washing his hands in the washroom. As he is drying his hands he suffers a pain in his chest and sucks in his breath. In some haste he takes a small bottle of pills out of his pocket, swallows two and drinks from the cold water tap to wash them down. Pause. He looks at himself in the mirror and grimaces.*

He combs his hair, adjusts his suit, walks through to the sitting room. He puts a record on a gramophone. It is a jazz cornet piece. ZHDANOV *looks at his watch, sits down, lights a cigarette and listens to the music. He concentrates hard, frowning, puffing on his cigarette.*

PROKOFIEV *arrives at the door to the sitting room. He is using a stick and is obviously in some distress. He is beautifully and correctly dressed. Steadying himself, he pauses, listening to the music which he can hear through the door. He smiles as he recognizes it. He waits, then shrugs and knocks at the door.* ZHDANOV *does not hear the knock above the music.* PROKOFIEV *knocks on the door with the handle of his stick.*

ZHDANOV: Enter!
> (PROKOFIEV *straightens himself up, opens the door and enters, closing the door behind him.* ZHDANOV *looks at him but says nothing.* PROKOFIEV *stands in front of* ZHDANOV *like a soldier before his commanding officer, not daring to move. He leans heavily on his stick. He looks at* ZHDANOV *half enquiringly, half pityingly, as if trying to guess the reason for* ZHDANOV'S *bad manners.* ZHDANOV *suddenly gets up and takes the needle off the gramophone.*)
> So much for your reputation as a punctual man, Prokofiev.

PROKOFIEV: I arrived on time but I managed to get lost in the building. There are a lot of stairs.

ZHDANOV: I left instruction for you to be taken to the lift. No matter. You're here. That music mean anything to you?

PROKOFIEV: Bix Beiderbecke, I think.

ZHDANOV: (*Looking at the record*) Leon Bismark Beiderbecke according to this. Not very Germanic in tone. Obviously a man who has betrayed his origins.

PROKOFIEV: May I sit down?

ZHDANOV: Yes.

(PROKOFIEV *sits down. Pause.* ZHDANOV *looks at his watch again.*)

Someone told me that you'd had a bad fall.

PROKOFIEV: That is correct.

ZHDANOV: You should look where you're going.

PROKOFIEV: I blacked out, actually.

ZHDANOV: It's a wonder I don't black out being stuck at the Musicians' Union Conference for days on end. Can you imagine what it's like suffocating in a room with hundreds of bloody musicians and composers, trying to get some sense out of them. What a time I've had.

PROKOFIEV: I'm sorry that I cannot join you.

ZHDANOV: Can't or won't?

PROKOFIEV: It would be my duty to be there if I were capable of making a contribution.

(SHOSTAKOVICH *arrives at the door and knocks immediately.*)

ZHDANOV: Enter!

(SHOSTAKOVICH *enters and closes the door behind him. He appears anxious and slightly pugnacious as though expecting to fend off an attack.*)

The least that we might expect from a musician is that he should keep good time.

SHOSTAKOVICH: This place is a warren.

ZHDANOV: Not full of rabbits though.

SHOSTAKOVICH: Sergei, how are you? Don't get up.

PROKOFIEV: Much better, thank you.

ZHDANOV: Well, Comrade Shostakovich, you can fill in your colleague about what progress we are making at the conference. That shouldn't take long, should it?

PROKOFIEV: That would be useful if I'm to understand the basis for this evening's discussion.

ZHDANOV: Discussion? (*Laughs.*) I like that. Discussion. Go on, Shostakovich. Shoot! We have a few moments to spare before he comes.

SHOSTAKOVICH: Well, let's see. We have spent a lot of time on Muradeli's opera, *The Great Fellowship*. Comrade Zhdanov, as the chairman of the conference you may see it differently but I would say that we are using Muradeli's work as a test case, analysing it . . .

ZHDANOV: Not by itself. It has been coupled with your own masterpiece, *Lady Macbeth of Mtensk*, these two works being the most unpopular operas written in Russia for fifty years.

SHOSTAKOVICH: I didn't hear anyone making that observation.

ZHDANOV: Didn't you? Well, I'm making it now.

SHOSTAKOVICH: (*To* PROKOFIEV) Did you hear Muradeli's opera when it was first produced?

PROKOFIEV: No, I missed it, unfortunately. What is it about?

SHOSTAKOVICH: Where shall I start? It's set in Georgia up in the mountains. It's about the period when the Soviet Government was being established there.

PROKOFIEV: I see.

SHOSTAKOVICH: The Party's land reform programme is opposed by some wealthy farmers . . .

ZHDANOV: At unexpected moments the whole orchestra starts blaring! During lyrical interludes the drums suddenly burst in! In the middle of heroic passages he plants sad, elegiac, winsome themes. Muradeli is mad. And you're no better.

PROKOFIEV: I would like to have heard this discussion. Did the conference come up with any answers?

SHOSTAKOVICH: The Art Committee and its chairman, Comrade Khrapchenko, were partly blamed. Muradeli blamed himself and his musical education. Some interesting facts emerged. I didn't know, for instance, that three hundred operas have been written in the Soviet Union in the last thirty years. Nor that the price of harps was so outrageous.

ZHDANOV: You and your friends have confused the entire music brotherhood of the Soviet Union. Only one man can sort it out now. But, I ask you, should we be wasting his time?

SHOSTAKOVICH: At least we will find out what he thinks.

ZHDANOV: I've been telling you what he thinks! I am his spokesman on all cultural matters!

SHOSTAKOVICH: Do you know what he actually thinks of my work, himself?

ZHDANOV: You're going to find out shortly.

SHOSTAKOVICH: Has he any respect for it?

ZHDANOV: Have you?

SHOSTAKOVICH: Have I? I have to live with it.

ZHDANOV: (*To* PROKOFIEV) Do you respect his work?

PROKOFIEV: I know that he is always interested in constructive criticism. When and if I am in a position to provide some I will make it available in a serious, respectful way.

ZHDANOV: You talk like you write music—backwards!

(*Pause.* ZHDANOV *looks at his watch. He is getting even more irritable with anxiety. He lights another cigarette.*)

PROKOFIEV: Is there anything we should know before he arrives? I have never met Comrade Stalin. I am not even sure of the correct way to address him.

(STALIN *enters the washroom through a hidden door. He is carrying a flat, rectangular parcel. He closes the door and goes through to the toilet. Putting the lid down on the pedestal he sits on it. For a moment he looks very tired. Leaning the parcel against the pedestal he gets to his feet and looks in the mirror. Taking a small comb from his pocket he combs his moustache, his eyebrows and his hair. There is something almost womanly about the way he does this.*)

ZHDANOV: His official titles are: Father of the People; the Greatest Genius in History; Friend and Teacher of all Toilers; Shining Sun of Humanity; and Life-Giving Force of Socialism—but you say what you like. Why not call him Cloth-Ears?

PROKOFIEV: I would appreciate your advice. What is the proper form?

ZHDANOV: Comrade Stalin is the form. The same as anyone else. Kiss his big toe if you want to.

PROKOFIEV: All this trouble over a little music. It is shameful that we have to bother him about it.

(STALIN *starts singing in the washroom as he combs his thick, black hair. Its colour has a hard, unnatural gloss to it.*)

STALIN: (*Singing*) He who clothes himself with light
as with a garment,
stood naked at the judgement.
On his cheek he received blows
from the hands which he had formed.
The lawless multitude nailed to the Cross
the Lord of glory.

(*As soon as* ZHDANOV *hears the first bars of the song he leaps to his feet and listens.*)

ZHDANOV: That's him! He's coming.

(*Pause. The three of them look at the upstage door.* SHOSTAKOVICH *and* PROKOFIEV *realize that the sound is coming from elsewhere and look at the other door which leads to the washroom.* ZHDANOV *follows suit.*)

How did he get in there?

SHOSTAKOVICH: What's in that room?

ZHDANOV: A lavatory. He's in the lavatory. What the hell is he singing about?

PROKOFIEV: It's the old Easter hymn. Don't you recognize it?

(*The singing stops. Pause.* STALIN *sits on the pedestal again, picks up the parcel and clutches it to his chest. Pause.* ZHDANOV *listens intently.* STALIN *reaches up and pulls the chain.* ZHDANOV *smiles, relaxes a little.*)

ZHDANOV: Sounds like one of your string quartets.

(STALIN *gets up and leaves the washroom, turning the light out as he goes.*)

Look lively now.

(STALIN *enters. He goes straight to the mantelshelf and props the parcel up on it.* PROKOFIEV *is struggling to get out of his chair.* STALIN *presses him back.*)

STALIN: Sit down before you fall down. You don't look well. What's your doctor like?

PROKOFIEV: Good evening, sir. My doctor is competent, I believe.

STALIN: I doubt it.

PROKOFIEV: I hope, for my sake, you are wrong.

STALIN: Oh, I can be wrong. Health is a very personal matter. The foundations of a sound constitution are laid in childhood—the air we breathe, the environment. Andrei here had a bad doctor. He wasn't helping him at all, was he?

ZHDANOV: No.

STALIN: He was killing him—neglect, ignorance. So Andrei is now being treated by my doctors—all seven of them. I'm so healthy that they've got nothing to do so they're keeping their hand in with Andrei. He's a real challenge to them. A very complicated case, aren't you?

(STALIN *goes to a painted wall and opens up a hidden cupboard that is packed with bottles of vodka of different colours.*)

Who's drinking? Not much food here. A few nuts and biscuits. I would have invited you to dinner but I had another engagement. Are you hungry? You look well fed. (*He roots in the drinks cupboard looking at the bottles.*) It's years since I was in this room. Who was I with last time? Can't remember. What shall we try tonight? Ah, there's more of this than the others. The yellow one. Is yellow our colour, Comrades?

(STALIN *holds up a bottle of zubrovka-flavour vodka. Idly he tosses it to* ZHDANOV *who is nearly caught off guard. He immediately starts to open it.*)

You like the smell of grass in your vodka? No, you two are more for pepper, I should think. Or big, fat, glossy plums. But we can start off with the zubrovka. The flavour of horse fodder.

ZHDANOV: I don't think I'll have any. It's bad for my heart.

(*Pause.* STALIN *pours himself a glass of vodka and knocks it back. Pause. He looks meaningfully at* ZHDANOV.)

STALIN: I don't want any nonsense from you, Andrei.

ZHDANOV: Your doctors say I shouldn't.

STALIN: What do they know about it? Doctors think everything is bad for you. Do you know how I've stayed so fit? Ignoring doctors and eating gooseberries. Are you drinking, Shostakovich?

SHOSTAKOVICH: Yes, please.

STALIN: And you, my well-travelled man?

(PROKOFIEV *smiles uncertainly*.)

PROKOFIEV: I am forbidden alcohol.

STALIN: The bottle is here if you change your mind. This is very pure, you know? The best. What can we give you? I'll get some tea later. You like tea, don't you?

PROKOFIEV: Please don't go to any trouble. I dined before I came here.

STALIN: Very cold. Not a night to be out. I hope you wrapped up well. Always protect the throat. That is a crucial area. And wear a good hat. Well, this is very pleasant. My dinner was good fun.

(STALIN *sits down*. ZHDANOV *follows suit*. SHOSTAKOVICH *sits down*.)

Old friends. We reminisced. Old friends are the best. We were at school together. The laughs we had in those days. It is good to share food with old companions, maybe cry a little. We sang a few songs from the old days. I wonder if you'd know them?

(*Pause. He looks at* SHOSTAKOVICH, *then at* PROKOFIEV.)

Did you have a good Christmas?

SHOSTAKOVICH: Quiet.

STALIN: My old friends brought me a present. I haven't opened it yet.

(ZHDANOV *pours out three glasses of vodka and hands one to* STALIN *who takes it and stands by the mantelshelf.* ZHDANOV *looks at* SHOSTAKOVICH, *then at the glass of vodka. He has no intention of serving him with it.* SHOSTAKOVICH *takes the glass.*)

Let's guess what it is. You first.

(STALIN *nods at* SHOSTAKOVICH.)

SHOSTAKOVICH: May I pick it up?

STALIN: Why not?

(SHOSTAKOVICH *picks up the parcel and weighs it in his hands*.)

SHOSTAKOVICH: Reasonably heavy.

STALIN: Reasonably heavy. Not metal?

SHOSTAKOVICH: No. Too light for metal. Maybe wood.

STALIN: What about you, Prokofiev?

PROKOFIEV: Could it be a book?

STALIN: Imagination at work. A book. What do you say, Andrei?

ZHDANOV: Has it been examined?

STALIN: Don't be so officious, man! This was a Christmas present! Old friends bought it with their own money, carried it all the way to Moscow.

ZHDANOV: It should have been examined.

(*Pause.* STALIN *takes the parcel off* SHOSTAKOVICH *and walks purposefully over to* PROKOFIEV, *putting the parcel into his hands, then retreating a few paces.*)

STALIN: Open it for me.

(*Pause.* PROKOFIEV *smiles.* STALIN *moves to the other side of the room.*)

PROKOFIEV: Don't you like opening presents? I love it. It's the anticipation. What can it be? Something I've always wanted or . . . handkerchiefs, socks, an awful tie . . .

(PROKOFIEV *unwraps the parcel. It is an icon. He holds it up. Pause.* STALIN *smiles, nods, goes over to* PROKOFIEV *and tenderly takes the icon out of his hands. He laughs out loud.*)

STALIN: Fancy them knowing that I needed an icon. A very thoughtful present.

(*He gives it to* ZHDANOV *to look at.*)

What do you think?

ZHDANOV: Seventeenth-century Georgian. Excellent workmanship. A very true, firm style. Simple but effective.

STALIN: Do you see the artist there? No. Not a trace. He has submerged himself in his work. No individual screaming to get out. What is the subject?

SHOSTAKOVICH: Christ in glory.

PROKOFIEV: Or Christ in judgement. Perhaps they are the same thing. I can't remember.

STALIN: Keep the difference in mind. You'll find that it helps. Now, the men who brought me this beautiful gift all the way from Tiflis are all well over a hundred years old. They are my old tutors from the seminary. I thought they'd all be dead but no. Relics from the nineteenth century. Saints in the making.

PROKOFIEV: That is remarkable.

STALIN: I thought so. Those three old men to take that terrible journey in winter! Astonishing. I didn't even know they were coming. I find that very touching. To go to such trouble for a boy who failed to do what they wanted him to. That is truly noble.

(STALIN *throws back his vodka and gives his glass to* ZHDANOV *who refills it.* STALIN *takes it and nods to* ZHDANOV *to drink his own.* ZHDANOV *unwillingly obeys.*)

(*To* SHOSTAKOVICH) Play me the best thing you've ever written.

SHOSTAKOVICH: I'm not sure what that is.

STALIN: Have another drink first.

(STALIN *fills* SHOSTAKOVICH's *glass, then stands by the piano.* SHOSTAKOVICH *goes across, frowning apprehensively.*)

SHOSTAKOVICH: Much of my best work is symphonic in form, I'm afraid.

STALIN: Scale it down.

SHOSTAKOVICH: Well, that would take time . . .

STALIN: A tune! Play me a tune! Don't quibble.

SHOSTAKOVICH: I'm not quibbling, I'm just trying to explain.

STALIN: You're as nervous as a girl on her wedding night. What's the matter with you? I thought this was your profession? You just stroke the keys with your fingers.

(STALIN *plays a few notes.*)

Is this thing in tune?

SHOSTAKOVICH: Near enough.

STALIN: Andrei!

SHOSTAKOVICH: It's all right.

ZHDANOV: The central heating affects the wires.

STALIN: And what a rubbishy old piano. Can't we afford something better than this? I'm sorry, Shostakovich. I'm asking you to perform on an inferior instrument. A genius of your calibre should have a Steinway. This isn't good enough for you. No tone. No style. No resonance.

(STALIN *plays a run of notes. One of them is a thud.*)

What's that note? (*Plays it again and again.*) Sounds like something very avant-garde. (*Opens up the piano and looks down. Putting in his hand he pulls out a letter.*) Someone has

17

been using our piano as a post-box.

(*He reads the address on the letter, then hands it to* ZHDANOV.)

Who is it addressed to?

ZHDANOV: Someone's wife. I think I remember his face.

STALIN: It must be a farewell letter. See that the wife gets it. Better late than never. Now, let us enjoy some beautiful, soul-stirring music. I feel ready for that.

(STALIN *takes* SHOSTAKOVICH *by the shoulders and firmly presses him down on the piano stool.*)

Only a little tune. Show me what you can do.

SHOSTAKOVICH: Don't you laugh, Sergei.

STALIN: He won't. He's next. Come on, we have a lot to get through. Wait. Wait. I want to ask someone for something. (*He goes over to the icon.*) Let this boy pass his examinations. He has worked hard. We have paid for lessons for him, made sacrifices. People have gone without food or shelter so this boy can learn his music. The whole family has done without so young Dmitri can be a great composer and make us proud.

(*Pause.* STALIN *looks at* SHOSTAKOVICH *who remains still and quiet at the piano, waiting. Pause.* SHOSTAKOVICH *makes a false start then sits back.*)

SHOSTAKOVICH: Sorry.

STALIN: Don't worry. Nerves. Pretend that never happened. Start again.

(SHOSTAKOVICH *plays a theme from his Concerto No. 1 for Piano, Trumpet and Strings, Op. 35.* STALIN *pours himself another drink.* ZHDANOV *is getting very angry, glaring at* SHOSTAKOVICH. STALIN *puts a hand on his arm and indicates that he should remain cool.* PROKOFIEV *leans his forehead on the knob of his stick as if listening, or praying.* SHOSTAKOVICH *builds up his piece from a lulling, slow movement into a tremendous finale and finishes. Pause.* STALIN *blows an enormous raspberry.*)

Thought you'd like an extra instrument at the end.

SHOSTAKOVICH: I did score a trumpet in the piece itself. You instinctively recognized the need for it.

STALIN: When did you write that?

SHOSTAKOVICH: Ten years ago.

ZHDANOV: It's an insult.

STALIN: Don't be so emotional, Andrei. Ten years ago. Another age. Before the war. I can hardly remember what it was like to be alive then, so much has happened. What did you think of that piece, Prokofiev?

PROKOFIEV: There was a certain tension in the playing that I found worrying.

STALIN: Not the playing. The piece.

PROKOFIEV: It is part of a larger work.

ZHDANOV: You know that work as well as I do. You've had to sit through it. Come on, you're a man, aren't you? You've got a mind of your own. What did you think of it? (*Pause.*) I'll say one thing. The members of the Musicians' Union certainly stick together.

PROKOFIEV: We were well taught. In unity is strength.

(STALIN *chuckles. Pause.* SHOSTAKOVICH *rises hesitantly from the piano stool, hoping his ordeal is over.* STALIN *stares at him and he subsides.* STALIN *grins, then beckons him to get up.* SHOSTAKOVICH *leaves the piano.*)

STALIN: Now, I'm ignorant about some music. You three are all from good, solid bourgeois backgrounds. You should understand that kind of tricksy, intellectual creation we've just heard. What did it mean?

ZHDANOV: It didn't mean anything.

STALIN: Andrei gives in straight away. Come on, you can do better than that. You must have spent hours on a Sunday in the front parlour listening to bourgeois music, making bourgeois music. This is very much your field.

ZHDANOV: We never listened to shit like that.

STALIN: What did you listen to?

ZHDANOV: Er . . . I don't know . . . my father wasn't all that musical . . .

STALIN: A Tsarist Inspector of Schools not musical?

(STALIN *taps out a rhythm on the piano top with his glass.*)
Know what that is?

PROKOFIEV: Two four time?

STALIN: My father was a shoemaker.

(*Pause.* STALIN *pours himself another drink.*)

When he was drunk, which was often, he used to amuse himself playing different rhythms on his last as he repaired the shoes of the bourgeoisie. And he'd sing as he worked well into the night. I used to lie in my bed under his bench, listening. I can still sing all those old songs. But no matter how long I listened to your music, Shostakovich, I would never remember the melody. Do you know why?

ZHDANOV: Melody? He's never heard of it. There is no melody.

STALIN: Let him answer.

ZHDANOV: We've been through all this at the conference. Everyone has condemned his kind of formalist, progressive crap.

STALIN: In his greatest moments Shostakovich writes music which we accept as the emotional language of Soviet reality.

(*Pause.* SHOSTAKOVICH *smiles a wintry smile.* ZHDANOV *is puzzled.* PROKOFIEV *can hardly suppress a laugh.*)

One cannot but be proud of a talent so unique, so original, so universally significant.

ZHDANOV: Ha! That sly, boot-licking critic, Asafiev. (*To* SHOSTAKOVICH) How much did you pay him?

STALIN: You don't get out of it that easily, Andrei. In September 1944, the Central Committee of the Party—on which you sit—proclaimed this young man's *Leningrad Symphony* to be a work of genius of the first magnitude. As you were the commander of our forces at Leningrad, Andrei, perhaps you felt grateful that Shostakovich had made you immortal?

ZHDANOV: No one can think straight in wartime. We've had a chance to consider it since. I'll say one thing. He did write quite a good tune for that symphony. And do you know what he did? He gave it to the German army. It was their theme. Bam–bam–bam as they hammered on the gates of Leningrad.

PROKOFIEV: If one had been a cat in the siege of Leningrad, one would have been eaten, so I hear.

ZHDANOV: You weren't there, of course. What were you doing in the war, comrade? Building barricades across the door of your salon?

(*Pause.* STALIN *sits at the piano.*)

STALIN: You know that your friend, the critic Asafiev who wrote such a glowing tribute to your work, is in the process of changing his mind about it?

PROKOFIEV: Will you excuse me for a moment?

(PROKOFIEV *struggles to his feet. No one goes to help him. He leans heavily on his stick and crosses to the washroom door.* STALIN *plays a theme on the piano.* PROKOFIEV *goes into the washroom and shuts the door, locking it. Leaning on the basin he shakes his head, then runs cold water into it and splashes his face.*)

STALIN: (*To* SHOSTAKOVICH) You are in very serious trouble.

SHOSTAKOVICH: What have I done?

STALIN: You are in more trouble than any of the others—more than poor, old Prokofiev, Khachaturyan, Miaskovsky and that lot. Do you know why?

SHOSTAKOVICH: I have no idea.

STALIN: Because you are younger. You are the future.

(PROKOFIEV *is suddenly violently sick.*)

SHOSTAKOVICH: Please do not think me impertinent, but every one of the composers you have mentioned, including myself, have been showered with Stalin Prizes year after year. There is no more room on my mantelpiece.

STALIN: Do you believe in prizes? Do you believe in all that fawning? How many members of the Stalin Prize Committee do you still see in high office? Or any office. What do you think of this theme?

(STALIN *plays it again.* PROKOFIEV *sits down on the lid of the pedestal, his head in his hands. After a while he lights a cigarette.*)

SHOSTAKOVICH: What is it?

ZHDANOV: I thought you knew everything about music. The darling of the Conservatoire.

STALIN: Haunting, isn't it?

SHOSTAKOVICH: Prokofiev is a long time in the washroom.

(STALIN *slams the lid of the piano down and stalks away.* PROKOFIEV *hears the crash and reacts.*)

STALIN: That was insulting, Shostakovich, very insulting!

SHOSTAKOVICH: I'm sorry. I don't know the piece.

STALIN: It's mine. I just made it up. I looked at that beautiful icon with all its memories, its history of suffering, and that music came into my head. I saw old Hermogenes, the principal of the seminary, a very stiff, stern old man, and I wondered what had happened to him.

(*Pause.* SHOSTAKOVICH *pours himself another vodka. He knocks it back.* STALIN *smiles.*)

I'm sorry. No man should think that he can do everything. Look at Andrei. He has too many jobs to do. He is crippled with overwork. I feel for him. Chairman of the Foreign Affairs Committee, chief of the propaganda department, military councillor for the Red Navy . . . and culture? He is the supremo, the top man. The Inspector of Schools rides again.

(PROKOFIEV *finishes his cigarette and throws the butt down the pan. He flushes it away.*)

ZHDANOV: A lot of thinking has been going on in there. Let's hope he's got rid of all the shit he was going to write during the next few years.

STALIN: How is your wife, Irina? Your son, Maxim? Your daughter, Galya? All well?

SHOSTAKOVICH: Yes.

STALIN: There is too much sickness around. Naturally we are healthy animals. I'm tired of ill people. I would like to see everyone with bright eyes and rosy cheeks.

(PROKOFIEV *enters. He looks very shaky.*)

Help him.

(SHOSTAKOVICH *goes to support* PROKOFIEV.)

Not you.

(ZHDANOV *helps* PROKOFIEV *to a chair.*)

ZHDANOV: He's been sick. I can smell it on his breath.

PROKOFIEV: I'm sorry.

STALIN: Where did you eat dinner?

PROKOFIEV: At home.

STALIN: No one would want to poison you, would they? Perhaps the meat was off. Did you have meat?

PROKOFIEV: I am very nervous.

STALIN: No matter what happens, a person should have control of his eating. The stomach and the mind are strongly interconnected. You are an emotional man. That is a good quality.

PROKOFIEV: Thank you.

STALIN: Why did you refuse to attend the Musicians' Union Conference?

PROKOFIEV: I didn't refuse. My doctor said that it would not be advisable.

STALIN: What's the matter with you, anyway?

PROKOFIEV: A stroke. I am still recovering. It is a nuisance.

STALIN: But you are here. If you can come here, why can't you attend the conference?

PROKOFIEV: I was not given an option.

STALIN: That's right. And Comrade Zhdanov was wrong to give you an option not to attend the conference. I'd have had you carried in on a stretcher. You're a very important man. The conference is crippled because you're not there. How can they take a decision of any sort without the senior Soviet composer? You will go tomorrow.

PROKOFIEV: You flatter me, sir.

STALIN: Andrei, I want to be notified the moment this man enters the conference chamber tomorrow morning. If he needs an ambulance, send one. Give him a sedan chair if he wants one. Rig up a cable car!

PROKOFIEV: I'm very tired.

STALIN: I'm older than you, and look at me. People live a long time where I come from. We have sound, peasant constitutions—clean, wholesome food, fresh air. You spent too much time in Paris and New York as a young man. Your liver is wrecked. (*Pause.*) Here, you might as well drink. It will keep you going. It's as good as medicine any day.

(STALIN *puts a glass of vodka in* PROKOFIEV's *hand and stands over him.*)

PROKOFIEV: I would rather not.

STALIN: It will do you no harm.

PROKOFIEV: I'm not allowed stimulants.

STALIN: Don't lie to me. The truth is that you don't drink vodka. Your preference is for French and German wines. I hear

23

that you have a special affection for champagne.

PROKOFIEV: I've been drinking vodka all my life.

STALIN: Let's see you drink it now then.

(PROKOFIEV *sips the vodka. He smiles up at* STALIN.)

PROKOFIEV: Excellent quality.

STALIN: Only the best. I'll give you a toast. To the power of the human heart.

(STALIN *clinks his glass with* PROKOFIEV *and beams down at him.*) I am very disappointed in the work of the Musicians' Union Conference so far. All we have had is back-biting, boot-licking, ancient professors covering their tracks, everyone sucking up to the Chairman and the Central Committee, saying what they think I want to hear. It has been a travesty of open, democratic discussion. No one will take the plunge. All they're good for is following the Party line. That's no use to me. I thought, in my innocence, if all those creative people are stuffed into one room and made to think hard, they'll come up with some new ideas for Soviet music, some useful ideas. How wrong I was. They hadn't got the guts to reach out and claim what was theirs. Now I've got to do it for them.

ZHDANOV: Many of the delegates said . . .

STALIN: I don't want to hear any more sycophantic drivelling!

ZHDANOV: All I was going to say is that everyone is grateful for the time and trouble that the Central Committee is taking over music—not the most obvious of our priorities.

STALIN: Good of them. To me music is as important as heavy industry or agriculture. It has got to work.

SHOSTAKOVICH: I think some good things have come out of the conference . . .

STALIN: Confessions, complaints, throat-cutting. I've read the transcripts each day.

SHOSTAKOVICH: I thought that the point about the peoples of the Soviet Union having more than a hundred languages and nearly as many musical styles was a good one; we have the four-voice music of the Ukrainians, the seven-note scale of Azerbaijan, the five-note scale of the Tartars and the Buriat Mongols . . . the variety is enormous. How do we forge one

24

national music out of all these without destroying something?

STALIN: Your musical hearing will have to become as acute as my political hearing.

ZHDANOV: I think the conference has also agreed that bad, disharmonious music undoubtedly has a damaging effect on the psycho-physiological activity of the brain. The part of the brain that controls hearing also controls balance and vomiting. So, you two are making everyone physically sick as well as mentally ill. You probably brought on that stroke yourself, Prokofiev—listening to your own music.

PROKOFIEV: My own doctor has said that if I keep on composing music it will kill me. I wonder if he meant the same thing?

STALIN: When the conference is over, the Central Committee is going to issue a decree. The decree, in itself, will be a piece of paper if I don't get the support of men like yourselves.

PROKOFIEV: We are both loyal citizens.

STALIN: But not loyal composers. Read them the decree.

ZHDANOV: (*Taking a paper out of his pocket*) This will be issued in the second week of February. (*Reads*:) The Central Committee of the Communist Party decrees that:

1) the formalist tendency in Soviet music is anti-people and is leading to the liquidation of music.

2) Soviet composers must become more conscious of their duties to the People and stimulate the kind of creative activity that will lead to higher quality works being composed which will be worthy of the Soviet people.

3) a proposal should go forward to the Propaganda and Agitation Department of the Central Committee and the Government Arts Committee that the state of affairs in Soviet music must be improved and its present faults liquidated.

PROKOFIEV: Am I a present fault?

ZHDANOV: You are. And a formalist tendency.

SHOSTAKOVICH: I would like to study that document more closely. Some of the ideas are quite complex. . . . (*He gets agitated.*) Well, I can't say that I understand what it's getting at! Have you any idea what it means? May I have a good look at it? I honestly want to be . . . clear. Comrade Stalin . . . was that anything to do with me? I'm mystified. Conscious of my duties? I've never been anything else.

STALIN: Let me see that.

(ZHDANOV *hands him the decree.*)

How many times have you drafted this?

ZHDANOV: Ten, at least.

STALIN: It still sounds very clumsy, Andrei, very clumsy. It's jargon. You know how I feel about language. You mustn't mangle it.

SHOSTAKOVICH: And aren't you jumping to conclusions if you've written that before the conference is over? I thought that's what we were supposed to be discussing. We haven't made any recommendations yet.

ZHDANOV: (*In a fury*) D'you think we're going to wait until you bloody idiots make up your minds? That could take till doomsday!

(*Pause.* SHOSTAKOVICH *looks hurt and puzzled.*)

SHOSTAKOVICH: Well, all I can say is that it won't be worth us reporting our findings to the Central Committee if you've already made up your minds.

ZHDANOV: (*Trying to keep his temper*) The conference has been a bloody calamity from beginning to end! It's been going round in circles!

STALIN: (*Gently*) This is just a short cut, Shostakovich—a technique that statesmen must use when they're under pressure. I agree with you that it goes against the grain but there we are. Time is precious.

SHOSTAKOVICH: Well, I suppose you know best. I was just thinking of all the hard work we've put in at the conference. Never mind. Will we still be allowed to make our report?

STALIN: Of course. It will be read with great interest, I assure you.

SHOSTAKOVICH: Good. You never know, we might come up with something.

ZHDANOV: And pigs might fly. This decree will have the same force as law, Shostakovich. Anyone who goes against it will be punished.

PROKOFIEV: How will we know when we are writing works not worthy of the Soviet people?

STALIN: Well, have you got an answer to that? It's a fair question.

ZHDANOV: (*Pause.*) When you don't live up to . . .

PROKOFIEV: Expectations? Aspirations?

ZHDANOV: Don't put words in my mouth!

PROKOFIEV: In practice people tell us what they think of our work by coming to hear it or staying away. Even that is not completely reliable, however. People are not always right.

ZHDANOV: The People aren't always right? Go on, go on.

PROKOFIEV: That may sound like heresy but many great works were very unpopular when first performed. People were hostile to them for decades. Some composers have to wait a hundred years or more while the public comes round to giving them recognition. By then, of course, the poor fellows are dead and gone.

STALIN: That's worth thinking about. Even the greatest lives are snuffed out, made into total failures. It's hard, very hard. And it's so random. How d'you feel about it?

PROKOFIEV: One has to be fatalistic.

STALIN: Do you worry that there remains much of your best work left undone? Perhaps that preys on your mind? You must sit at home, looking into the future. Doesn't it get you into a grim kind of mood? You stop. You disintegrate. Everything melts away. What could be left is nothing but lies. Have you spent your life well?

PROKOFIEV: A lot of time has been wasted. As a young man I got side-tracked quite a lot. However, there were compensations. (*Pause.*) Life isn't over yet.

STALIN: Surely you don't think that you're going to get better? Once you've had one stroke . . .

PROKOFIEV: (*Sharply interrupting* STALIN) I will deal with that myself, thank you!

STALIN: You're right. With will-power anything is possible. You want to carry on, staggering along?

PROKOFIEV: I can't think what else I'd like to do. Somehow it

27

remains entertaining.

STALIN: Shostakovich has his best years ahead of him, and his health. There's hope for him. But what about you?

ZHDANOV: You must have had many moments of despair. I would in your position. Nothing to look forward to. You're probably drying up.

SHOSTAKOVICH: That's not so, he's just written . . .

ZHDANOV: I don't know why you bother to hang around.

STALIN: Leave him alone.

(*Pause.* PROKOFIEV *stares* ZHDANOV *out.*)

Andrei's had an uphill fight with culture. It enrages him sometimes. Don't forget, he is a dedicated man. If he feels antagonism towards you it will be on a matter of principle, not personal.

(*Pause.* STALIN *looks at the decree again.*)

This is an admission of defeat, really. That aspect of it offends me. But you have to feel for them, Andrei. Music is not an exact science.

(STALIN *continues examining the decree.*)

ZHDANOV: Don't tell me. (*Pause.*) I don't think we need to take up too much of your time tonight. It is my opinion, and the feeling of the conference, that all that is needed is a purposeful, practical approach based on our success in reorientating other areas of the arts. First, we'll have to have a complete clean-out . . .

SHOSTAKOVICH: May I ask when this was discussed at the conference? I've been there all the time but I've never heard anyone bring that up.

ZHDANOV: I said that was the *feeling* of the conference! (*Pause.*) We did it with literature. We did it with painting. Film. Even poetry. There are no problems left in those areas. Only music is holding us up. (*Pause.*) Delegates have come to me privately and said that the influence of Prokofiev and Shostakovich is too great for any other composer to take a new step forward. They hold people back. In their own way, they are dictators.

PROKOFIEV: That is a ludicrous suggestion!

ZHDANOV: You can appreciate how difficult it is for any other

composer at the conference to get up and speak his
mind. He feels that he will be jeopardizing his position with
Shostakovich and Prokofiev. After the conference is over he
still has to earn his living. With the power that these two
wield in the music establishment they could destroy him.
So, they come to me off-the-record, as it were. They are
very disturbed.

PROKOFIEV: May we know who these disturbed people are?

ZHDANOV: They want that kept a secret.

PROKOFIEV: In case we victimize them?

ZHDANOV: Makes sense, doesn't it?

SHOSTAKOVICH: They're mad! If they haven't got the courage to
say this to our faces you shouldn't take it into
consideration.

ZHDANOV: We take everything into consideration. (*Pause.*) Music
has to be swept clean if there's to be any real chance of
progress. That's what people want. And I think they're
right.

STALIN: I must say that I wasn't aware that these two had
become so unpopular amongst their own kind. That is
worrying. Of course, achievement often excites envy. A very
human failing, I'm afraid.

ZHDANOV: They reckon they're untouchable!

STALIN: You don't think you're untouchable, do you?

PROKOFIEV: Only in the Indian sense.

STALIN: Whether you like it or not, these two are the greatest
composers in the world! No, it's you I'm disappointed with,
Andrei. I like to delegate but people like you let me down.
You're supposed to be a well-read, cultured, civilized man
but you appear to have no common sense. You can't talk to
these men in a language that they understand. Anti-people?
What does that mean to them? Have they ever even heard
of the Propaganda and Agitation Department? Why should
they have? And the liquidation of music! That is a term
that is well beyond their comprehension—and mine,
incidentally.

ZHDANOV: They know what I'm getting at.

STALIN: Are either of you two paid-up members of the

29

Communist Party?

SHOSTAKOVICH: I didn't think we had to be . . .

STALIN: Don't get so defensive. I was only asking. Prokofiev?

PROKOFIEV: No, I'm not.

STALIN: Have either of you ever read Marx? Does he mean anything to you?

PROKOFIEV: I tried to read *Das Kapital* when I was a student.

STALIN: But it defeated you. Perfectly natural. Only someone with a truly scientific and philosophical mind of the highest grade can tackle that monster. I have read it from cover to cover. Andrei must have conquered it. Eh?

ZHDANOV: Took me three months. It was worth every minute.

STALIN: They may be the experts on music, you see, Andrei—but we are the philosophers. This is the problem. To get our vision into their heads. Given the choice, Prokofiev would prefer some kind of liberal government, wouldn't you?

PROKOFIEV: I generally restrict my choices to what is available.

STALIN: You can be honest with me. Communism is a scientific creed. We can't expect artists to understand it without our help. That's what I'm trying to do—help you. Tell me what political party you would join if you had the chance, Shostakovich.

SHOSTAKOVICH: I don't think about it much . . .

ZHDANOV: Best you keep it that way. Josef, you won't get anything out of them on this tack. We know that neither of them have ever been politically active. They're ignoramuses. It wouldn't make a scrap of difference to them if they lived under capitalism or communism. They don't want to serve anyone's ideas but their own. Politically they're made of jelly.

STALIN: If I arranged for special classes—one of our top theoreticians—that might help. Some of them are very good teachers. How about that, Prokofiev? In the time that you've got left on this earth—which can't be long—you could get to grips with the beauties of scientific communism. It's a garden of delights—take my word for it.

ZHDANOV: He'll say yes but he won't mean it. He's a cynic right through to the core. His motivation has always been self, self, self. It's too deeply rooted in his make-up to get it out now. It takes guts to reach down and purify yourself, get all the dirt out . . .

STALIN: Why can't these two do that? You managed it somehow.

ZHDANOV: Josef, we're talking about being reborn by an effort of will. That's what you have to go through. All your old, false values have to be destroyed. They haven't got the slightest intention of changing. They think they're perfect.

PROKOFIEV: Perhaps Comrade Zhdanov would give us lessons in self-denial?

(*Pause.* ZHDANOV *stares coldly at* PROKOFIEV.)

ZHDANOV: There're quite a few lessons I'd like to give you, Prokofiev. (*Pause.*) Don't you realize what you are? Like me you were born into a rotten, decadent class. But I got out. Not you. You still like it. Being a parasite is right up your street.

PROKOFIEV: Is that why I came back to Russia?

ZHDANOV: Parasites need things to live off.

PROKOFIEV: I can assure you that being a parasite is much easier in the West. I could have lived out the rest of my life there on the reputation that I had by 1932. We have heard about your struggle—are you interested in mine?

ZHDANOV: Russia means nothing to you.

PROKOFIEV: (*Angrily*) It is my home!

ZHDANOV: Your home? Your playground, you mean!

PROKOFIEV: What else must I call the place where my family, my friends live? You talk about being reborn. There are personal ways to achieve change in oneself. Some people can do it faster than others. It is not always a straightforward matter.

ZHDANOV: Nothing ever is with you. (*Pause.*) A family man, eh? Such devotion. Pity you can't spare some of that for your country.

PROKOFIEV: I am devoted to my country. I always have been.

ZHDANOV: Married a Spaniard. Not important, I suppose. It just demonstrates an attitude of mind. Not surprising though. He's of Polish extraction himself, I've heard. A foreigner.

Yes, Prokofiev's almost an immigrant, really. (*Pause.*)
Give my regards to your mistress. Does she count as
family? Or don't I understand Bohemian life?

(PROKOFIEV *takes a measured pause to control his anger.*)

PROKOFIEV: My wife's father was Spanish. That I confess though
I fail to see that it can be held against her, or against me.
But I am not in any way Polish. I am pure Russian. All my
grandparents were Russian. Also, I am not a Bohemian but
I do share their views on the need for freedom in one's
personal feelings. Do you have such things?

ZHDANOV: That's a crack I'll hold to your account.

PROKOFIEV: Always paid my bills. To honest tradesmen, at least.

ZHDANOV: Say that again!

PROKOFIEV: I try to avoid repeating myself.

STALIN: I think it would help matters if you tried to get on. You
must watch your tongue, Prokofiev. Keep to the business in
hand.

PROKOFIEV: That is my wish.

STALIN: Come on, this is a professional matter. I don't want any
silliness. You were very provocative, Andrei. What do we
care about his wretched love life?

(ZHDANOV *refuses to be moved. He glares at* PROKOFIEV, *then turns
away as if preventing himself from making a physical attack on him.*
STALIN *pats him on the shoulder to soothe him down.*)

ZHDANOV: The hypocritical, bourgeois bastard is getting at me! I
won't have it!

STALIN: Andrei! That's enough now! You're spoiling our
evening.

ZHDANOV: I can't stand being in the same room as him! Send
him out!

PROKOFIEV: Not yet, be fair. I've been quite looking forward to
doing my party piece. Dmitri did his stuff at the piano. So
should I. You know how vainglorious I am. Any
opportunity to show off. Just put me at the centre of
attention and I'm happy. Don't you want me to sit my
pianoforte examinations?

STALIN: Quite right.

(*Pause.* STALIN *looks at* PROKOFIEV *with some approval.*)

You keep your head and remember things. I find that praiseworthy.

SHOSTAKOVICH: Yes, play for us, Sergei. I'd like to hear you. Play a good long piece. Really, I need to get my breath back. I don't know where I am . . .

PROKOFIEV: I doubt whether I'll be on top form tonight.

STALIN: Don't tell me your hands are shaking. You? Master of the keyboard?

PROKOFIEV: No, no. Just a passing phase. The body letting the mind down. I don't know. Well? Should I play? I'm quite happy to, really. It's up to you.

STALIN: No, I don't think so. My judgement must remain clear. You might make too good an impression on me. (*Pause.*) Even I am not impervious to charm, Prokofiev.

ZHDANOV: But I am. We know that you're a dab hand at the keyboard—oh, you're a very polished performer. What I'm interested in is the creature inside the natty suit when everything is quiet. No music. No amusing conversation. Just a little man thinking his thoughts. How about owning up to those?

(*Pause.* PROKOFIEV *looks straight ahead.*)

They call me old X-ray Eyes. (*Pause.*) Shostakovich was at a friend's apartment last week—funny friends he has, I might add—and someone—it might have been him—called you Genghis Khan the Second, Josef.

STALIN: Did they really?

SHOSTAKOVICH: That simply isn't true. Where do you get such stories from? Somebody must spend a lot of time making them up.

STALIN: Genghis Khan. Hm. Andrei, you mustn't tell me these things. The idea of artists making fun of me behind my back is very painful.

ZHDANOV: They say worse things than that. Little Hitler.

STALIN: Little Hitler? Not even Big Hitler. Now I do feel put out. This is so much tittle-tattle. You don't honestly expect me to take it seriously, do you?

ZHDANOV: You should hear them, Josef. They go at it hammer and tongs. Jokes, stories, we've even found cartoons they've

33

drawn. Look at these.

(ZHDANOV *gives* STALIN *a piece of paper. He studies it, nods. He keeps a perfectly straight face and shows it first to* PROKOFIEV *and then to* SHOSTAKOVICH. *They remain deadpan, almost like zombies, killing all expression in their faces.*)

STALIN: Har–har–har. Aren't I funny? Good old Uncle Joe. (*He makes the gesture of wiping his arse on the paper.*) Har–har–har.

ZHDANOV: The woman who drew those lived two floors above Shostakovich. She was a journalist.

(STALIN *hands the cartoons back to* ZHDANOV *who puts them away.*)

STALIN: Mickey Mouse. Donald Duck. What about Pluto? Why leave him out? Why did they give a stupid dog that name? Do you know who the real Pluto was, Shostakovich? He wasn't a Yankee dog at all, was he?

SHOSTAKOVICH: He was the Greek god of Hell, I think. But he had a dog.

STALIN: Trust the Americans to forget something like that. No sense of what fits, just belittling culture, ridiculing everything that is sacred. They contaminate thought, they poison the world. All they want is money. If I sent you to America on a goodwill mission, would you come back?

SHOSTAKOVICH: Of course. . . . The dog's name was Cerberus, by the way.

STALIN: Andrei, look into the eyes of these men. What do you see? Confusion. Something has been radically wrong with their schooling at all levels. Get me a list of everyone who has been responsible for their education.

SHOSTAKOVICH: Comrade Stalin . . . I've tried to make my own mind up about things . . . my teachers can't be held responsible for my failure . . .

STALIN: I'll decide that.

SHOSTAKOVICH: They did their best. I wasn't the perfect pupil by any means.

STALIN: If we agree—as I think we must—that you have either been corrupted or neglected—someone is to blame. I don't think it's you but you can persuade me otherwise if you wish. We will only ask these people a few questions about

34

the curriculum, their teaching methods, disciplinary problems that they might have had. Andrei can arrange this kind of investigation quite easily, using only skilled people. Rest assured that everyone's feelings will be respected. After all, a teacher can only do so much. What was Lenin's view of the Soviet artist in society?

SHOSTAKOVICH: Lenin's view . . . ah, yes . . . well . . . I'm sure it's familiar . . .

STALIN: Come on, have a go. You remember Lenin. The one with the bald head. Don't say you've forgotten him already.

SHOSTAKOVICH: No . . . it's just that my mind . . .

ZHDANOV: My mind. My mind. My this. My that.

SHOSTAKOVICH: Very well. I'll shut up then. I'm lost anyway.

STALIN: You are supposed to be the engineer of the soul. I can just see Prokofiev in his oily overalls with a spanner in his hand. One of the results of our great victory in the war has been that people are discussing the soul a great deal. It is a word on everyone's lips. The reason? We all felt that wonderful joy in victory. We asked ourselves what it was. What organ of the body made the sensation. It was the soul. It is in my mind to create a government department for the soul. (*Pause.*) Want the job, Andrei?

ZHDANOV: Not if you make me keep men like this on the books. You've listened to my suggestions before, taken action on them. We've cleaned out Soviet culture from top to bottom and it's ten times better for it. Why won't you listen to me this time?

STALIN: The Department of the Soul. Do you know, I think I'd give up my present responsibilities and take that on if people would leave me in peace. Prokofiev would work there, Shostakovich too. Although I would be their supervisor we would have a very close working relationship. We would lunch together in the canteen of the Department of the Soul. I like them, Andrei. As men, I like them. And they like me, I think. Do you like me?

PROKOFIEV: Yes. Very much.

STALIN: He does. Shostakovich is thinking about it.

PROKOFIEV: Dmitri is trying to do something very difficult.

35

STALIN: What is that?

PROKOFIEV: To separate the idea of you from the actual man. The awe and respect we feel for our leaders sometimes prevents us from appreciating them as people. But I think Dmitri has made up his mind.

SHOSTAKOVICH: I like you. We get on. That means a lot to me.

STALIN: What a relief. Well, that's three of us who like each other. We haven't involved Andrei yet. Do we like him?

ZHDANOV: Leave me out of it. These two know how I feel about them.

STALIN: Andrei, soften your heart. Tell me, old faithful, have you ever heard of the music of the spheres? Well, here we have two major planets which have fallen out of orbit, that's all. The sun must pull them back.

ZHDANOV: I want these two removed!

STALIN: Andrei!

ZHDANOV: Other composers will come along. Throw these two out! Get rid of them!

STALIN: That would be a waste.

ZHDANOV: If a gun's barrel gets bent you don't bother to try and straighten it out. It will never be the same again no matter what you do. So, melt it down and recast.

STALIN: That's very hard. Who ever bothered to put these two right? I never had the time, you were busy . . .

ZHDANOV: I'd set fire to their shirt-tails and use the bastards for target practice. I'd strap the sods over a cannon's mouth and blow their balls to Berlin and back!

STALIN: He doesn't mean that.

ZHDANOV: I do! I've given up with them. They're write-offs!

STALIN: Andrei, calm down. You know that artists are prone to suicide. And these are sensitive men.

ZHDANOV: Let them hang themselves. I couldn't care less.

STALIN: Don't be so defeatist. It's not like you. It's our job to make them happy. That's very important. They won't get into that state with old soldiers barking at them.

ZHDANOV: Yes, I'm a soldier, and proud of it. What's the matter with serving your country? Is it a crime?

STALIN: Not at all. But has it occurred to you that our friends here wish to serve their country as well?

ZHDANOV: Don't make me laugh.

STALIN: They do! The problem is—how? (*Pause.*) It's not as easy
to work out as a soldier's sacrifice. What a genius has got to
offer is something very special. Try to understand that.

ZHDANOV: I'll tell you what I understand, Josef! That when
you've marched five hundred thousand men into battle you
know all about how many beats to the bar. I've stood in
flooded trenches with farm boys who'd sing better than
opera stars when they could hear themselves above the
artillery. That was real music to my ears. And they didn't
ask for sympathy. But, I tell you, to me those simple
soldiers were special. They had a genius. But what do they
get from these two twittering arseholes? Crash! Bang!
Wallop! (*Hits the piano keys with his fist.*) A din worse than
the guns! (*Hits the keys with his elbows.*) Any old rubbish! (*Sits
on the keyboard.*) Crash! Bang! Wallop!

STALIN: I would give a lot to hear, just once, music that
transformed our recent history of suffering and heroism into
joy. Purge the misery, change pain into delight. Do a job
for our souls, boys. Isn't that what you're here for? To do a
job for our souls?

ZHDANOV: Music's in the blood! And my blood's red, not
dishwater. Yes, and good music makes me want to dance!
Come on, we'll show 'em, Josef! We can dance these two
lilies into the ground! Rum–ti–tum–tum!

(ZHDANOV *dances around* SHOSTAKOVICH *and* PROKOFIEV.)

STALIN: Andrei, your heart!

ZHDANOV: To hell with my heart!

(*They dance together. It is a cumbersome but impressive routine that
suggests years of practice at parties.*)

STALIN: What will your doctors say?

ZHDANOV: To hell with my doctors!

(*They dance with linked arms, then* ZHDANOV *breaks away into a
solo performance of a wilder dance.* STALIN *laughs, clapping and
egging* ZHDANOV *on.* ZHDANOV *gets carried away by the dance,
exultantly showing off. Suddenly he gasps in pain, clutches his
chest and stops.* STALIN *smiles grimly and nods. Walking away*

37

from ZHDANOV.)

STALIN: Someone knocking at your door, Andrei? Take a pill.

ZHDANOV: What pill? (*Disengages himself.*) What pill? I don't take
pills. Go on talking without me.

STALIN: Sit down.

ZHDANOV: No, leave me be!

STALIN: You look terrible.

ZHDANOV: Don't go on about it! (*Pause.*) It will pass. (*Beats at his
heart.*) Get back in your kennel, you old dog.
(*He encounters* PROKOFIEV'*s eye.*)
Well? What's the matter with you? What are you looking
at?

PROKOFIEV: Self-destruction has always been a mystery to me.

ZHDANOV: When I die, musician, what I leave behind will be
more than a few vibrations.

STALIN: Don't be so morbid, Andrei. Sit quietly for a moment.
That's an order. Get your breath back. We'll listen to some
gramophone records.
(ZHDANOV *sits down.* STALIN *goes over to the record cabinet.*)
What have we got of Prokofiev's in the collection?

ZHDANOV: All his work that's been recorded.

STALIN: That should keep us occupied. (*Looks in the cabinet and
looks through the records.*) You have been busy.

ZHDANOV: Do we have to? I'm not in the mood for any of that
stuff right now.

STALIN: Ah, I see, you have different versions of the same work.

ZHDANOV: Oh, yes—French recordings, British, German,
American—and our own. The Soviet ones are much
inferior, of course. . . . Feast your eyes, Prokofiev. There's
your world-wide reputation.

PROKOFIEV: You do seem to have gone to an awful lot of trouble.

ZHDANOV: The Western record companies are very selective, of
course. Unlike us, your devoted Soviet fans, they don't
record every piece of nonsense that you write. They only
like you in parts. But we love you *in toto.*

STALIN: Come over here.
(PROKOFIEV *gets up and moves across.*)
I want you to choose your favourite piece from this lot and

put it on the gramophone.

SHOSTAKOVICH: Sergei, if you tell me which piece you want played I'll find it for you and put it on.

STALIN: You stay where you are. Let him come and browse. Surely you've got the strength to put on a gramophone record.

PROKOFIEV: (*Moving across to the gramophone*) Oh, it will be difficult to choose. All my recorded work. Such a plethora.

SHOSTAKOVICH: Have you got a full collection of my work as well?

ZHDANOV: Ah, he's jealous. You artists. So vulnerable. Your pile is much smaller than Prokofiev's. The West has not developed such a taste for your music—yet. But there's time.

(PROKOFIEV *stands at the record cabinet trying to look at the collection. It is very awkward for him.*)

PROKOFIEV: I'm sorry to have to be such a nuisance, but I'm not supposed to do any bending over.

ZHDANOV: I thought you queens spent all your time bending over.

(PROKOFIEV *straightens up. He walks towards the door with as much dignity as his body will allow.*)

STALIN: Where are you going?

PROKOFIEV: I do not intend to stay here if he speaks to me like that.

STALIN: You are quite right. That remark was most uncalled for. Andrei will apologize.

ZHDANOV: Come on, it was only a joke. You know what they say about artists being pansies.

PROKOFIEV: And you know what they say about soldiers being brutal. May I make a joke about that?

(*Pause.* PROKOFIEV *eyes* ZHDANOV *defiantly.*)

STALIN: Have the grace to apologize to the man.

ZHDANOV: I'm sorry, Prokofiev. Please forgive me.

PROKOFIEV: Thank you. I would like to go home.

STALIN: No. Choose your record.

PROKOFIEV: It is impossible for me to think clearly under these circumstances!

STALIN: (*Conducting* PROKOFIEV *back to the record cabinet*) Andrei
will behave himself from now on, I promise you. Now, let's
all have another drink and relax. Listening to music should
be a pleasure.

(*Pause.* PROKOFIEV *reaches the cabinet. He tries to bend but cannot.
He raps on the floor with his stick in frustration.*)

PROKOFIEV: Really, I can't manage this . . .

STALIN: Why don't you sit on the floor to look at the records?
Wouldn't that be easier?

(STALIN *gives* PROKOFIEV *his arm.* PROKOFIEV *bows his head.*
STALIN *half forces him down as a nurse might do with a recalcitrant
patient.* ZHDANOV *laughs softly and pours out more vodka.*
SHOSTAKOVICH *turns away, very upset.* STALIN *remains standing
over* PROKOFIEV.)

Georgia is the place for artists. You would feel happier
there, Prokofiev. Georgia is our Soviet Mediterranean. As a
colonial myself I have to make the point that you Russian
men of culture don't have to go sniffing round the sewers of
Rome, Athens, even Moscow to get the smell of civilization.
We have it all there in my homeland. Balconies with
trailing vines. Rolling wheatfields. The Caucasus
mountains. Yes, I'm thinking very seriously about the idea
of a camp for all the artists in the Soviet Union to be set up
in Georgia. You'd enjoy that, wouldn't you?

PROKOFIEV: Sounds lovely. This really is a very good collection,
Dmitri.

(PROKOFIEV *looks through the collection, trying to look as relaxed as
possible.* ZHDANOV *sits on the piano stool, glaring down at him.*)

ZHDANOV: Found anything yet?

PROKOFIEV: It's terribly difficult to choose. I don't play my own
music back on records very much. I feel a little shy.

ZHDANOV: You wrote the stuff. You must have some idea what
bits of it have any value. Does getting your hands on that
pile give you a thrill, Prokofiev? Does anything matter but
fame?

PROKOFIEV: It might be more appropriate for you to ask
Comrade Stalin that question.

(STALIN *bursts out laughing and caresses the top of* PROKOFIEV's *head.*)

STALIN: Good boy, you tell him. Always stick up for yourself.
Don't let Andrei bully you around. (*Sits next to* PROKOFIEV *on
the floor.*) What have we got here? *Alexander Nevsky. Ivan the
Terrible. War and Peace.* What a good Russian you are.

ZHDANOV: Know my favourite piece of yours, Prokofiev? *Peter and
the Wolf.* It appeals to my childish mind. Da–da–da–da–da–
da–da . . .

STALIN: *Romeo and Juliet.* Young love. Shakespeare was a randy
devil I hear. He went to bed with Queen Elizabeth. Sorry,
we're not allowed to mention the word queen. What's this?
The Duenna. Never heard of that. What's it about?

ZHDANOV: It's based on a play by an English playwright called
Sheridan.

STALIN: Another English playwright? Hm.

PROKOFIEV: Irish, actually.

STALIN: Ah, that's different. Obviously he was a revolutionary.
Didn't he inspire the Celts to resist British imperialism?

PROKOFIEV: Sheridan lived in London for most of the time. He
wrote comedies about eighteenth-century social life.

STALIN: Criticizing the aristocracy and the repressive capitalist
regime.

ZHDANOV: Yes, yes, all that kind of thing. Prokofiev wouldn't
have decided to adapt it otherwise, would he?
(PROKOFIEV *holds up a record.*)

PROKOFIEV: I've made my choice.

STALIN: Let me see.
(PROKOFIEV *hands* STALIN *the record. He studies it.*)
The Footsteps of Steel. Ballet music. Never heard of it. Has it
ever been produced?

PROKOFIEV: The subject is the Machine Age. It was first
produced in Paris in 1927 by Diaghilev.
(STALIN *is helping* PROKOFIEV *to his feet. At the mention of
Diaghilev they go still. A short, cold pause.*)

STALIN: Diaghilev had something to do with this thing?

PROKOFIEV: Yes. We seemed to work quite well together most of
the time. We had our differences.

ZHDANOV: I should hope you did. Diaghilev refused to work in

Russia. He was a traitor.

PROKOFIEV: As a producer of ballet he had a lot of style.

STALIN: And he betrayed his country with a lot of style. (*Breaks the record on his knee.*) Sorry we can't play your choice. What else have we got here?

(STALIN *takes another record out of its sleeve.*)

Ah, your Fourth Piano Concerto. There must be some merit in that. Let's hear what it sounds like.

(*He smashes it. He takes another record.*)

The Classical Symphony. What a nice label. His Master's Voice. A little white dog. The English breed good dogs.

(*He smashes it, takes another record.*)

Your Second Symphony. Play this one for us. Andrei.

(STALIN *gives the record to* ZHDANOV. *He looks at it for a moment, smiles at* PROKOFIEV, *then smashes it against the furniture.* STALIN *empties the cabinet, handing the records to* ZHDANOV *who smashes them. They work swiftly, efficiently, like production workers on a machine line of destruction. Shostakovich's drum crescendo from the Eleventh Symphony takes over. Lights fade to blackout.*)

ACT TWO

Out of the darkness comes the drum crescendo of Shostakovich's Eleventh Symphony.

Lights swiftly up on STALIN *and* ZHDANOV *smashing records.* STALIN *hands a record to* ZHDANOV *who swings back his arm . . .*

STALIN: No! We'll play that one.

ZHDANOV: Come on! Let's do the lot!

STALIN: No, we'll play it. We should hear one, at least.

ZHDANOV: Let's finish the job!

STALIN: We'll take it as Prokofiev's choice—blind. He's a gambling man, aren't you?

ZHDANOV: What about Shostakovich's lot? We're going to do them as well, aren't we? It wouldn't be fair otherwise.

STALIN: My arm's aching.
   (*Takes the record back off* ZHDANOV.)
   Let's see what we've got here.
   (STALIN *puts the record on the gramophone. It is Bix Beiderbecke playing 'Old Man River'.* ZHDANOV *looks acutely uncomfortable.* STALIN *frowns.*)
   (*Shouting*) You wrote this?
   (PROKOFIEV *shakes his head. He cannot help laughing.* STALIN *takes off the record.*)
   What's going on here? Is somebody playing games with me?

ZHDANOV: I can explain, Josef. . .

STALIN: Is that someone's idea of a joke? What's that record doing here? How did it get in?

ZHDANOV: I'm trying to keep track of the black market in Western music. This stuff has been smuggled in for years. We're working on a case at the moment . . . I, er, had it with me when I arrived . . .

STALIN: And I thought poor old Prokofiev had written it! (*Roars*

43

with laughter, then stops. Pause.) Do you listen to that kind of thing?

SHOSTAKOVICH: It is my . . . business to keep abreast . . . I mean, it's very difficult to ignore anything . . . even music from . . . India or Japan, anywhere . . . Patagonia!

STALIN: You have to take drugs to listen to jazz. You took drugs?

SHOSTAKOVICH: No. I wouldn't know where to start.

STALIN: So where did you find this record, Andrei? In the shops?

ZHDANOV: In a writer's flat.

(STALIN *hands the record to* ZHDANOV.)

STALIN: You'd better take care of it then if it's evidence. But be careful where you leave things like that in future, Andrei. Prokofiev got the shock of his life, didn't you?

(STALIN *laughs and pats* PROKOFIEV *on the shoulder. Telephone rings.* ZHDANOV *walks over the broken records to answer the telephone.*)

ZHDANOV: Yes? What is it? I said we weren't to be disturbed. (*Pause.*) Oh. Not good. (*Pause.*) How many? (*Pause.*) Hm. That's rough.

STALIN: What is it? Hurry up and get off the line.

ZHDANOV: There's been a mining disaster in the Ukraine. The editor of *Pravda* wants to publish a message from you to the survivors in tomorrow's issue . . .

STALIN: Tell him that I'm too busy.

ZHDANOV: Four hundred and twenty dead.

STALIN: I can't deal with it now. Tell him I'm involved with something far more serious. Maybe I'll do a piece for the day after tomorrow. We'll see.

ZHDANOV: Try again tomorrow . . .

STALIN: Afternoon at the earliest.

ZHDANOV: Late afternoon.

STALIN: Say I'm working on something which is probably going to take all night.

ZHDANOV: It's an all-night session. Make it evening before he tries again.

(ZHDANOV *puts the telephone down. Pause.* STALIN *pours himself more vodka and takes a handful of nuts. He wanders round the room filling up the other glasses.*)

That makes me feel sick. Four hundred and twenty dead and we're stuck here yapping about music.

STALIN: What a barbarian you are, Andrei. There will always be miners, there will always be holes in the ground. But music sometimes drains away from an entire civilization. Do you know why? Because nobody cares about it.

(*Pause.* STALIN *goes over to* SHOSTAKOVICH.)

I think I'll give you a commission to write me a piece of music about this disaster in the Ukraine. It's a miserable, unhappy business and so it's right up your street. Why shouldn't you make a profit out of these miners?

SHOSTAKOVICH: (*Angrily*) Do you think I don't care about people?

STALIN: What are we short of in the Soviet Union? Miners or composers?

SHOSTAKOVICH: What is the matter with me? Come on! Let's have it. Tell me!

PROKOFIEV: Dmitri, calm down.

STALIN: No, let him shout. I'm glad to see his eyes flashing behind his bank clerk's spectacles. The blackbird is ruffled. This is what is the matter with you. You have forgotten this.

(STALIN *goes over to the piano. He sits down and accompanies himself as he sings a simple, melodic folk-song. It has a chorus which he encourages them to join in.* ZHDANOV *does so with gusto.* PROKOFIEV *and* SHOSTAKOVICH *make a half-hearted response.*)

That wasn't very good, boys. Come over here and sing it again. It's only a simple, peasant song. You keep quiet, Andrei. Let them do it alone this time. One. Two. Three.

(STALIN *leaves the piano and conducts as choirmaster.* PROKOFIEV *and* SHOSTAKOVICH *sing weakly and with reluctance.*)

Stop! What's the matter with you? You're sabotaging it, deliberately, you Russian snobs! Is a Georgian folk-song not good enough for you? Now, listen, you two. Either you come down off your pedestals or I'll have you shot. Do you understand? Shot. Andrei will take you down to the Lubianka prison and have you done first thing in the

45

morning. So, stop wasting my time. Sing it again and
put some feeling into it.

(PROKOFIEV *and* SHOSTAKOVICH *sing the song with more
animation. Half-way through* STALIN *starts to smile and joins in,
beckoning* ZHDANOV *to do the same.*)

Not bad, not bad. Now, we'll take the parts. Andrei, you've
got an ear that is too easily influenced by what you hear
around you. Stick with the tune and start the verse with
me. Prokofiev, try the baritone line. (*Gives him a phrase.*) Not
difficult. Shostakovich, I think you could manage the bass.
(*Gives him a phrase.*) It's not too low. If it is you can switch
to tenor. Improvise on it if you like. Let's see what we can
make of it. This first try is in the nature of an experiment,
boys. Here's our note, Andrei. Yours, Prokofiev; yours,
Shostakovich. One. Two. Three.

(*They sing the song successfully in parts.* STALIN *is delighted.*)

Very good! You see how easy it is? I'm very pleased
with that. Hearing that old song took me right back.
Can you hear the monks running to stop us? We should
have been singing hymns, not love songs. The piano
may not be used for any purpose other than the
practice of liturgical chants, anthems or, at the most,
cantatas. Josef Vissarionvich Djugashvili is not to be
permitted to use the piano again. He defiles it with
secular filth!

(STALIN *takes the icon and carries it around the room held high above
his head.*)

He will, for his punishment, carry the icon of our Lord in
glory above his head around the refectory ten times before
each meal and ten times after. No, not the one with the
wooden frame. The one with the frame of lead.

(*Pause. He stops and lowers the icon to cover his chest.*)

Now do you think that you have suffered more for music
than I have? I was always in trouble. You see, we were
forbidden to sing Georgian songs—simple, warm-hearted
songs that we had learnt at home. Why? Because they
tended to be about Georgian heroes, wild men, brigands,
fighters for independence. The Orthodox Church didn't like

46

that. Nor did the Imperial Russian Government. So, I ended up carrying Christ through the smell of boiled cabbage until my arm ached. But it was worth it, for music.

ZHDANOV: Those songs are worth suffering for. People can understand them. They belong to everyone. We don't even know who wrote most of them, they were composed so long ago. Or were they composed at all? Sometimes I think that word stinks. I think some music just comes out of people's souls.

STALIN: What do you know about Georgian songs, you ignorant lout?

ZHDANOV: I've heard them sung . . .

STALIN: Russian bastard! You can't speak a word of Georgian!

ZHDANOV: It's a difficult language.

STALIN: A dying language. I tell you, Andrei, there is more music, more beauty, more great literature in Georgia than anywhere else. But no one knows about it because it was stifled. I wasn't allowed to be taught at school in my own language. How do you think that made me feel?

ZHDANOV: Yes, what I'm saying is . . .

STALIN: Shut up.

ZHDANOV: There's no need for that.

STALIN: You get drunk very quickly.

ZHDANOV: I'm not drunk.

STALIN: Whenever I get reports from you—decisions you've made, things you've done, excuses you're making—I have to ask myself, has he been drinking?

ZHDANOV: That's not fair!

STALIN: It's common knowledge that you were drunk from one end of the siege of Leningrad to the other. Ask Shostakovich. Isn't that common knowledge?

SHOSTAKOVICH: I don't know.

STALIN: Don't be afraid of him. I sent him to Finland on a delicate mission. It needed diplomacy, tact. There was a lot at stake. What did he do? Drunk for weeks, getting his hand up girls' skirts, falling over at receptions, sleeping at meetings, vomiting in hotel foyers . . .

ZHDANOV: This is a lie!

STALIN: And you were heard talking French!! You fawning, snobbish, snivelling Francophone! You're like some bourgeois turd out of Chekhov. But you won't speak Georgian, will you? Why? Because it's the language of ordinary people who live natural, healthy lives—no affectations!

(*Pause.* ZHDANOV *is struggling to mind his tongue. He pours himself another drink and munches a biscuit.*)

I know I'll get more sympathy from my friends here than you, you arrogant Russian moron!

ZHDANOV: Whatever you say.

STALIN: These men are artists. They will know what I'm talking about. The agony of a nation made inarticulate. And don't sulk, Andrei. You drive me mad when you sulk.

ZHDANOV: I'm not sulking. I was thinking about what you have said. Why don't we revive the language? Build up awareness of its existence. Start a campaign.

STALIN: Make it artificial? If that is what you want, go ahead. It's a natural thing. It's to do with pride, history. How do you stimulate nature? Eh? How do you wake people up to what is being taken away from them?

(*Pause. He puts an arm round* ZHDANOV.)

He's all right. My oldest friend. One day he may succeed me, if he gets better. But I'll probably live to be well over a hundred, eh, Andrei?

(ZHDANOV *roars with laughter.*)

Give Jesus a drink.

(STALIN *holds up the icon.* ZHDANOV *puts his glass to the mouth of the figure. He tips vodka over it.*)

ZHDANOV: He doesn't want it. Not good enough for him. Perhaps he's developed a taste for vinegar.

(ZHDANOV *continues pouring vodka over the picture.* PROKOFIEV *watches with distaste but* SHOSTAKOVICH *is getting very agitated.*)

STALIN: I know more about this man, Jesus Christ, than any other person. Don't drown him, Andrei.

SHOSTAKOVICH: You're spoiling that!

ZHDANOV: What?

SHOSTAKOVICH: You're ruining it!

48

ZHDANOV: So what? Who's short of icons? Stupid bits of painted wood. Never liked them, always staring at me.

SHOSTAKOVICH: Don't you put any value on it? I thought it was a gift. Why are you letting him destroy it?

STALIN: It's well varnished. No harm will be done. Don't venerate it, whatever you do.

SHOSTAKOVICH: Someone painted it. Even the artist needs respect. Excuse me.

(SHOSTAKOVICH *stalks across the room towards the washroom exit.* ZHDANOV *bars his way. He holds up the icon and spits in its face.* SHOSTAKOVICH *is horrified.* PROKOFIEV *turns away.*)

ZHDANOV: Oh, what have I done? Sorry. Never spit into the wind. You never know who you'll hit.

(ZHDANOV *throws the icon on to the floor and bows* SHOSTAKOVICH *through.* SHOSTAKOVICH *goes into the washroom and closes the door. He leans on the wash-basin, head down, crying.* ZHDANOV *leans against the mantelpiece.*)

PROKOFIEV: Why do you make·yourself more ignorant and brutal than you are?

ZHDANOV: Don't talk to me, you lounge lizard.

PROKOFIEV: None of us can help our childhoods, where we came from.

ZHDANOV: Don't use that tone to me. We won a war, not a game of whist. It's about time that boy grew up. Sensitive about a bit of wood. What about him feeling for ordinary people instead of rubbish like that? And you as well, you intellectual. If I'd have pulled a poor man in off the street and spat in his face you'd have thought it was great fun. So much for your finer feelings.

(ZHDANOV *sits down at the piano.*)

What do you think this is? (*Tinkles the keys.*) It's just a big, black icon that sings. It's another of your holy objects. I saw you when you first came into this room. You didn't look at me. You looked at the piano. Well, you know what I say: people before pianos, people before Prokofiev.

PROKOFIEV: But not, and I may be guessing, people before politics.

ZHDANOV: What do you know about politics? You've spent most

49

of your life throbbing in a greenhouse. You're a tomato, a green tomato, even an impudent tomato. Perhaps I'll string you up.

(SHOSTAKOVICH *washes his face and hands very thoroughly, almost obsessively.* ZHDANOV *starts to play the piano, which he does surprisingly well. He grins at* PROKOFIEV *and* STALIN.)

SHOSTAKOVICH: I must not lose my temper.

ZHDANOV: Who wrote this? Keep quiet, Prokofiev, you're an expert. Let him guess.

SHOSTAKOVICH: I must stay cool and make as little comment as possible.

ZHDANOV: Come on. Who wrote it?

STALIN: Keep playing. I've heard it before.

SHOSTAKOVICH: Just survive, Dmitri, survive.

ZHDANOV: I'll give you a clue. (*Plays a flourish.*)

STALIN: Glinka.

ZHDANOV: No! Glinka? Never!

(SHOSTAKOVICH *washes his hands again and again.*)

STALIN: Skriabin.

ZHDANOV: Do me a favour!

STALIN: You're playing it badly. I can't tell.

PROKOFIEV: I disagree. He's making a fair attempt, I'd say.

ZHDANOV: You've no idea, have you?

SHOSTAKOVICH: I won't let them break me. I won't.

STALIN: Well, it's not Rimsky, it's not Tchaikovsky . . .

ZHDANOV: It's that mad Pole, that bloody mad, lecherous, lunatic Pole, Chopin! Failed, Josef Vissarion Djugashvili. Go to the bottom of the class. See, you assumed I'd only be able to play a Russian composer. But I'm a Renaissance man, a universal man.

(SHOSTAKOVICH *enters. He looks at* ZHDANOV *who is still seated at the piano.* ZHDANOV *winks at him.*)

Hello, Comrade. Did you hear me playing? Go on, say that you thought it was a gramophone record of Arthur Rubinstein. Go on, flatter me.

SHOSTAKOVICH: The walls here are very thick. I didn't hear it.

ZHDANOV: I was quite good for a stupid soldier. I can play the piano, but can you fight?

SHOSTAKOVICH: I can fight.

ZHDANOV: Good. How about you, Prokofiev? Do you want a fight?

PROKOFIEV: Not in my best form at the moment but if someone will hold me up I'll have a go.

ZHDANOV: Good. That's what I like to hear.

STALIN: I reckon these two would tackle anything. They're good men. You'll have a go, won't you?

PROKOFIEV: Of course. We always have, as you might have noticed.

ZHDANOV: Steady, musician.

STALIN: The man is right. I have noted their efforts. (*Pause.*) But they have not been good enough. So, why don't we get down to it and write the definitive new Soviet music together?
(*Pause.*)

SHOSTAKOVICH: Sergei and I have different styles . . .

PROKOFIEV: Hold on, Dmitri. Do you mean that we should collaborate on something? Why not? We might be able to make it work. It will take time. Perhaps we could spend a couple of weeks together in the country? I'll look in my diary and see what time I've got free.

SHOSTAKOVICH: Yes, by all means.

STALIN: No! That is not what I meant! To ask you two to collaborate would be futile. You are so vain and envious of each other that it would be doomed to failure. I'm told that you don't even like each other all that much. (*He opens the piano lid and plays a couple of notes.*) No, the four of us here tonight: me, Andrei, and you two, are going to compose something together.

ZHDANOV: A co-operative venture. Yes, it's a very good idea. We can make it work. I like the sound of that.

PROKOFIEV: Without wishing to be obstructive, Comrade Stalin . . .

STALIN: You refuse?

PROKOFIEV: No. I was just wondering if we might have some time to mull over the idea.

ZHDANOV: You've had plenty of time already. You've failed. If you'd done your job properly this wouldn't be necessary.

PROKOFIEV: I'm certainly not against experiments as such. Nor is Dmitri, I know. We both believe in a flexible approach. (*Pause. He looks at* SHOSTAKOVICH.)
If this is what you would like to do . . . we will help all we can.

STALIN: Good, Andrei and I are not unconscious of the privilege we are about to enjoy. Few people will have shared your extraordinary minds at such close quarters. Let us hope that we poor amateurs are not sucked in and lost without trace. (*Pause.*) Do you know Rustaveli?

PROKOFIEV: I've read him in translation.

STALIN: The greatest of Georgian poets. We are going to set one of his stories to music; the kind of music that you two should have been writing.
(*Pause. He looks at* SHOSTAKOVICH.)
Do you always have to look so unhappy?

SHOSTAKOVICH: I was thinking of the technical problems.

STALIN: What are they?

SHOSTAKOVICH: Music is a very personal language.

ZHDANOV: It doesn't have to be so private. You must learn to share. I'm a man, like you. You tell me what you're after and I'll tell you what I'm after.

SHOSTAKOVICH: But we're only dealing with sounds. That's very primitive. It can't be broken up, it's too basic . . .

PROKOFIEV: I think we'll have to judge the level of seriousness that the composition strikes very accurately. What it must do is suggest the . . . brotherliness of this venture . . . er, it will need an emotional balance that implies sharing, good nature . . . humour . . .

STALIN: Rustaveli is a very serious poet. I'm not having him trivialized.

PROKOFIEV: No, no, that isn't what I meant. Let me see . . . the mood of the piece should communicate this fusion of . . . different minds with a common goal . . .

STALIN: Yes, I see the sense in that.

PROKOFIEV: So, it must not be too individually tempered. After all, a group will always behave differently from a single person. Wouldn't you agree, Dmitri? For instance a crowd laughs more, because it is together. You must have noticed that in audiences, Dmitri.

(*Pause.* SHOSTAKOVICH *nods.*)

STALIN: He still looks unhappy.

SHOSTAKOVICH: No, I'm adjusting my mind to the idea. Yes, I think we can make something of this! Why haven't we tried it before? What will they say at the conference when this gets out? They'll be amazed.

PROKOFIEV: We couldn't have it ready for the last day, could we? Imagine playing it to them, the looks on their faces. By the way, I haven't brought any manuscript paper. Have we any?

STALIN: Everything we say is being recorded. We can go back over the tapes when we've finished and put the final score together. I've only got a few hours to spare so we will have to work quickly. (*Takes a paper from his inside pocket.*) Here's the story that we have to set to music. We can start.

PROKOFIEV: May I ask a question?

STALIN: Certainly, go ahead.

PROKOFIEV: Have we decided whether this composition is to be a ballet, an opera, a song-cycle, concerto?

STALIN: What do you think?

SHOSTAKOVICH: Let's hear the story first, then choose the form that will suit it best.

ZHDANOV: Good idea. Let's see what we're dealing with first.

STALIN: From *The Knight in the Tiger's Skin* by Rustaveli. Are you ready? The speaker is Tariel, the knight himself: 'As I came up the hill, the lion and tiger came walking together like a pair of lovers.'

ZHDANOV: Bom–bom–bom–bom, oh-ho!

STALIN: Andrei, just hold back your creativeness for a moment. We need to get the story firmly in our minds. Keep quiet until I've finished.

ZHDANOV: Sorry. I got carried away.

STALIN: 'As I came up the hill, the lion and tiger came walking together like a pair of lovers. Then they began to fight as

lovers do. The tiger fled with the lion in hot pursuit.
Then they sported gaily, then fought fiercely, neither
seeming to have a fear of death. Then the tiger lost heart,
even as women do, and ran away. The lion followed and tore
at her unmercifully. This displeased me. "Art thou out of thy
wits? Why dost thou persecute thy beloved?" I shouted,
rushing at the lion with my sword and spear. We fought and
I killed him, freeing him from this world's woe. Then I threw
away my bloody sword and embraced the tiger, wishing to
kiss it on the mouth, my mind full of hot longings for my
beloved whom I had left behind. The tiger roared at me and
chewed my face so I killed it in rage and frustration, beating
and dashing it to the ground, whirling it around my head,
remembering my nights of passion with my beloved.'

(STALIN *smiles and puts the paper on top of the piano. Pause.*)

SHOSTAKOVICH: Well, plenty to be going on with there, eh,
    Sergei?

PROKOFIEV: A rich field indeed.

SHOSTAKOVICH: It has great musical potential.

STALIN: You're not just saying that, are you? You can hear what
    I can hear inside it. When I first read the piece it rang in
    my head for days. I couldn't get it out of my mind.

SHOSTAKOVICH: Can you remember the key it rang in?

STALIN: No. I should have tried to establish it but there was no
    piano available. I was in prison.

SHOSTAKOVICH: Oh . . . I see.

PROKOFIEV: Should the music be martial in character?

STALIN: Partly.

PROKOFIEV: With the greatest of respect to your intense, personal
    experience, we must have a key to work with—even if it is
    only a starting point . . .

STALIN: Let me be quiet for a moment. (*Pause.*) Isn't it strange? I
    spent days humming the sounds that I heard in that piece.
    It nearly drove me mad. Couldn't sleep, couldn't think
    about anything else. Now I've forgotten. What a pity.

(PROKOFIEV *strikes a chord on the piano.*)

PROKOFIEV: B flat major. How about that?

SHOSTAKOVICH: I don't think there's enough emotional resonance in B flat major, Sergei. This is no ordinary knight on a walking holiday. This is man . . . at a very fundamental level of feeling. Am I right, Comrade?

STALIN: You are. (*Blows his nose.*) I don't fancy B flat major.

PROKOFIEV: Would you like me to play through all the major keys until we find the right one? I am presuming that it couldn't possibly be in a minor. (*Pause, then, with a touch of mischief*) Or atonal.

ZHDANOV: Under no circumstances. Would you like that, Josef? All the keys?

STALIN: Yes. Don't ever mention atonal to me again, you noisy child!

PROKOFIEV: The style of the melody must be governed by the mood of the words, and its shape by their sense and meaning. Are we agreed on that?

STALIN: I'm glad you mentioned a melody. And I don't want it ballsed up! D'you hear? I don't want you taking it to pieces and kicking it around until it's unrecognizable! Let's hear these keys.

(*Pause.* PROKOFIEV *starts to play through a series of major keys. He pauses at the end of each and looks questioningly at* STALIN. STALIN *waves him on each time.* PROKOFIEV *finishes and sits back.*)
Go on!

PROKOFIEV: That's the lot. We've run out of keys. There wasn't one that touched you?

STALIN: It was so long ago.

SHOSTAKOVICH: May I make a suggestion? To me there is a sadness in the violence of the story. It is Love and Death, the primitive and the civilized, conflicts that are acutely painful. Could we not consider the minor keys? They are very expressive of tragic conflict.

STALIN: No! You're dragging us down to misery again, you melancholy bastard! Make it . . . that third one you played . . . what was it? Near enough, near enough.

PROKOFIEV: An excellent choice. (*Plays the chord.*) G major, as I live and breathe. G for Georgia. G for gorgeous. G *not* for avant-garde! This is wonderfully liberating, Dmitri. Right. I say we should have a French horn for the tiger and a trombone for the lion.

STALIN: No trombone. I don't like trombones.

ZHDANOV: Cut the trombone.

SHOSTAKOVICH: Could it be a brass trio? We could have a tuba for Tariel.

STALIN: I don't want a trio.

ZHDANOV: The trio is out.

STALIN: This isn't going to be something a few street musicians can play. It's an important piece so it has to have majesty, power. And I don't want a tuba for Tariel. It's too fat.

SHOSTAKOVICH: The knight, Tariel, is on a journey.

ZHDANOV: Without his tuba.

STALIN: A journey, a pilgrimage, a quest.

SHOSTAKOVICH: Ah. Questing music.

PROKOFIEV: In G major.

ZHDANOV: What is it you don't like about trombones?

PROKOFIEV: Let's find the melody. We can orchestrate later.

STALIN: Man's life is the theme. The journey. When the journey stops in the body but goes on in the mind. Do you know when that is? Prison or old age. This is what it's all about, Andrei. We're getting through to them at last!

PROKOFIEV: Of course, we'll need a striped theme for the tiger.

ZHDANOV: How the hell do we do that?

STALIN: Oh, it's possible, possible. Keep your ears open.

PROKOFIEV: (*Illustrating on the piano*) There's black and yellow music. Music that eats one up. Man-eating music. How am I doing?

ZHDANOV: Got any tartan music while you're at it?

STALIN: Andrei! Stop being such an old sourpuss. This is great stuff!

PROKOFIEV: Rhythm, Dmitri.

SHOSTAKOVICH: Well, first part *walking up the hill*, wasn't it? That will have to be *andante*, and I imagine that Tariel, being a knight, would be clanking up the hill in a suit of armour. So it seems that a clanking *andante* is what we're looking for. As he's probably quite fit he could keep up a simple quadruple rhythm of four minim beats in the bar. Or is that too fast?

STALIN: Georgian knights never clanked.

56

SHOSTAKOVICH: Oh. Wrong again.

ZHDANOV: We don't want any clanking in this. Or farting. Or train sounds or nasty factory whistles! Understand!

STALIN: Georgian knights never clanked. They were too brave to wear armour. Next to their skins they wore silk. And they were very fit.

PROKOFIEV: If they wore silk they'd rustle. That could cause problems. If we do some rustling it might be taken as a hint that it's autumn with lots of leaves lying around. What time of year is it, by the way?

STALIN: I like the human voice.

SHOSTAKOVICH: An opera? Even Mozart couldn't write one in a single night.

PROKOFIEV: A song-cycle?

STALIN: Pooh.

SHOSTAKOVICH: Well, something for a large choir . . . a cantata.

STALIN: Thousands of voices. Thousands and thousands. In parts. That's what I want. You've hit it. Well done, what's your name.

ZHDANOV: Now we know where we are. That's a good choice. A huge cantata.

STALIN: A great work for the massed choir. Voices, melodies flowing in and out of each other. Just voices.

SHOSTAKOVICH: Then we will need the story to be adapted. We have to have the words in a manageable rhythm. At the moment they are all over the place.

STALIN: I'll be in charge of the words. Have you forgotten I'm a poet? It takes a poet to understand a poet. I was publishing verses before I was twenty. This will pose me no problem at all. Thousands of people singing it. Millions perhaps. All together.

ZHDANOV: What am I going to do?

STALIN: Keep our glasses filled and hand round the nuts.

ZHDANOV: I thought we were all supposed to be composing this.

STALIN: You can be the continuity girl.

PROKOFIEV: Shall we get started? I suggest that everyone makes what contribution they are capable of. May I ask what kind of personality this knight, Tariel, has?

57

ZHDANOV: Sounds a mad bastard to me.

STALIN: Complex. Fiercely independent, yet basically a humble man who wishes to help others. He is virtuous but often appears to be evil because of the actions forced upon him by circumstances. Although a simple man who understands love he has a struggle to equate it with his duty to his people. He has great physical strength and moral courage. Tariel is a true hero.

(*Pause.*)

ZHDANOV: How tall is he?

STALIN: What does that matter?

ZHDANOV: I need to see him in my mind's eye. If he was a dwarf . . .

STALIN: He's not a dwarf, idiot. Heroes aren't dwarfs!

PROKOFIEV: How about this? Walking up the hill, rustling along. Sun shining. A jolly nice day.

(*He plays a merry, mindless, fast tune.*)

STALIN: I've changed my mind. I don't like this song-cycle idea.

SHOSTAKOVICH: This isn't a song-cycle. It's a cantata.

STALIN: You never hear of song-cycles in folk music. You never hear of cantatas in folk music.

SHOSTAKOVICH: We can't just sit down and write folk music.

ZHDANOV: Why not? We're folk, aren't we? Are you saying we're not folk? I'll punch your face in!

STALIN: I'm folk, for one.

ZHDANOV: So'm I.

STALIN: Are you? I'm more folk than you are. I'm more folk than any of you. To be honest with you, I'm the ultimate folk. (*Pause.*) Prokofiev. Do you know what's left of you that is folk? The grave that is waiting for you. All your pretensions will drop away, my son. We'll dig you in like a spadeful of shit.

(*Pause.* PROKOFIEV *nods, smiles.*)

PROKOFIEV: You would like us to imitate folk melodies? So, my pretensions must continue. If I'm not folk, as you assure me I'm not, I must adopt a pose. (*Pause.*) It is a pity in music if we are not what we are, but . . . I can play the knight. I can play the peasant.

STALIN: All right, all right! Let's do this folk cantata. I'll adapt some of *The Knight in the Tiger's Skin*.

ZHDANOV: If you say so.

STALIN: You'll have to take it down as I recite it. It's a section that I learnt by heart. While passing it through my mind I'll improve it slightly. Just give me a moment to myself.

ZHDANOV: I hope you'll be able to read my writing.

STALIN: Shut up, you ox! (*Pause.*) Silence, please!

ZHDANOV: Sorry.

(STALIN *closes his eyes, concentrating hard.* ZHDANOV *stands by him with paper and pencil. The composers wait at the piano.*)

STALIN: I'm concentrating on the love theme, giving it an early development. What I thought might be a good idea is if the knight, Tariel, is thinking about his girl as he walks up the hill *before* he sees the lion and the tiger. So, he's striding along thinking the line: 'My woeful heart is like a caravan.'

PROKOFIEV: (*Pause. He frowns, shrugs, then improvises.*) 'My woeful heart is like a caravan'?

SHOSTAKOVICH: (*Improvising with him*) 'My woeful heart is like a caravan.' I think it would be stronger as: 'My woeful heart *is* a caravan.'

ZHDANOV: Then, how about: 'The wandering, trundling heart of Man'?

STALIN: Who d'you think you are? Rustaveli? The next phrase is—ah!

ZHDANOV: (*Writing it down*) 'Ah!'

SHOSTAKOVICH: 'Ah!'

PROKOFIEV: 'Ah!'

STALIN: 'To him who has been struck in the liver
        by a snake treacle is better suited
        than red candy.'

(PROKOFIEV *and* SHOSTAKOVICH *falter on the piano.* ZHDANOV *looks startled. Pause.*)

ZHDANOV: Would you mind giving us that again?

STALIN: 'To him who has been struck in the liver
        by a snake treacle is better suited
        than red candy. To him who is dying of poison
        antidote is everything.'

ZHDANOV: This is what is in the knight's head as he's climbing up the hill?

STALIN: Yes.

ZHDANOV: Mad bastard. Sounds as though he's suffering from a hangover.

STALIN: Just write it down, miss. Well, I think we've got a good beginning there. The mood should be reflective, like this. Move over.

(STALIN *pushes* SHOSTAKOVICH *off the stool and starts to improvise and sing.* PROKOFIEV *joins in on the piano.*)

'My woeful heart is a caravan.'

PROKOFIEV: 'My woeful heart is a caravan.'

ZHDANOV: Everyone's heart is a caravan. How the hell do we get from his heart being a caravan into his liver being bitten by a snake?

STALIN: Sssh. Try that again. 'My woeful heart is a caravan.'

SHOSTAKOVICH: Wouldn't it be a more workable line if we lengthened it to: 'My woeful heart is a caravan*serai*? Serai! Serai!'

STALIN: Show me.

(SHOSTAKOVICH *builds the theme into what they have composed so far.*)

PROKOFIEV: I quite like 'serai'. Do you like 'serai'?

ZHDANOV: I love it. What d'you want? Plain 'caravan' or 'caravanserai'?

SHOSTAKOVICH: I think tagging the 'serai' on to it would avoid any confusion. 'Caravanserai' means camels, horses. 'Caravan' could be motorized. That would make a different, non-medieval sound.

PROKOFIEV: No internal combustion engines in medieval Georgia. They hadn't invented it by then. Or had they? I'm quite happy to put one in. (*Plays an illustrative sequence.*)

STALIN: I think it should be 'caravanserai'. That's another two syllables on that line. 'Caravanserai.' Do we all agree?

PROKOFIEV: I'm perfectly happy.

SHOSTAKOVICH: I think we've voted that one in.

STALIN: Let's try this. (*Goes to the keyboard and develops a phrase.*) Good. Give me some of that walking music.

(*He plays as* PROKOFIEV *accompanies him.*)
'To him who is dying of poison.' Keep that serious.
(*They play again.*)
Set that. We're doing well. It's working, Andrei. It's
working. Let's try that, the four of us. Right. A few
footsteps of the knight coming up the hill as a kind of
prelude.
(*They play.*)
Then his romantic longings make themselves felt:

ALL: (*Sing*) My woeful heart is a caravanserai.
　　　　Ah! To him who has been struck in the liver
　　　　by a snake treacle is better suited
　　　　than red candy. To him who is dying of poison
　　　　antidote is everything.

STALIN: Let's hear what that sounds like. It felt all right to me.
ZHDANOV: Sergeant!! Play that back!
STALIN: What did you think, Prokofiev?
PROKOFIEV: I'd say we were breaking new ground, certainly.
　　　　(*A babbling screech of backwinding tape over the amplifiers, then the*
　　　　replay starts. The four of them listen intently. STALIN *is, at first,*
　　　　thoughtful, then incredulous, disappointed and dismayed in turn.
　　　　PROKOFIEV *and* SHOSTAKOVICH *watch* STALIN *wanly.* ZHDANOV
　　　　is visibly shaken but he keeps his eye on STALIN, *watching his mood*
　　　　worsen. The replay goes through to STALIN's *line*: Let's hear what
　　　　it sounds like. It felt all right to me. STALIN *reacts angrily.*)
ZHDANOV: That's enough, sergeant! Turn it off!
　　　　(*Pause.* STALIN *hangs his head.*)
STALIN: (*Without looking up*) Andrei!
ZHDANOV: (*Going over to him and leaning down*) Yes, Josef?
　　　　(STALIN *beckons* ZHDANOV *to come closer so he can whisper in his*
　　　　ear. ZHDANOV *listens, then straightens up.*)
Face the wall, you two!
　　　　(*Pause.* SHOSTAKOVICH *and* PROKOFIEV *obey, bewildered and*
　　　　apprehensive. STALIN *beckons* ZHDANOV *to lean down again. He*
　　　　whispers in ZHDANOV's *ear.*)
Certainly. Don't you go blaming yourself.
　　　　(ZHDANOV *goes round to where* PROKOFIEV *is facing the wall. He*
　　　　stands behind PROKOFIEV. *Pause. Taking a metal-topped pen out of*

his pocket he touches the back of PROKOFIEV*'s neck with it.*
PROKOFIEV *stiffens and almost cries out.*)

PROKOFIEV: What are you doing?

ZHDANOV: Give me your handkerchief. You have made Comrade
Stalin cry.

STALIN: That's right. I am crying.

ZHDANOV: He doesn't want you to see him like that. It makes
him feel ashamed. Not that he need be. It takes a man to
cry.

(ZHDANOV *goes back to* STALIN *with* PROKOFIEV*'s handkerchief.*
STALIN *takes it, wipes his eyes, blows his nose on it, then gives it
back to* ZHDANOV.)

PROKOFIEV: I'm sure we're all very sorry if we made you
unhappy.

STALIN: Give him his handkerchief back. I'm all right now.

PROKOFIEV: It isn't that serious . . . (*Turns.*) We can keep trying.

STALIN: (*Furiously*) Don't look at me. I'm very embarrassed.

(ZHDANOV *gives* PROKOFIEV *his handkerchief, deliberately opening
it up and smearing* PROKOFIEV*'s jacket as he sticks it back in his top
pocket.*)

I don't cry very often, so you see how crucial this has been
to me. It means that the deepest part of the emotions has
been disturbed. You have no idea how disappointed I am.

ZHDANOV: See what you've done? He reckons the whole thing is
his fault.

SHOSTAKOVICH: (*Still with his face to the wall*) We've only had one
go at it. There's a lot of rewriting to be done. That's where
most of the time and effort comes in. We'll just have to keep
hammering away until we get it right.

STALIN: D'you think that I want to hear thousands of Russians
singing that awful row? I never want to hear it again as
long as I live. How black everything's got. Do you go
through times like this?

SHOSTAKOVICH: Oh, often.

STALIN: You would. But I am not used to failure, boys. This has
been a very strange experience for me. (*Pause.*) They're not
laughing at me, are they, Andrei?

ZHDANOV: If they are I'll kill them with my bare hands.

STALIN: I don't mind if they look at me now.

ZHDANOV: Turn round! If I see smiles on your faces you're dead!
(SHOSTAKOVICH *and* PROKOFIEV *turn round.* STALIN *looks up at them and smiles. Pause.*)

STALIN: I wish I didn't get this way, boys.

ZHDANOV: Don't make excuses to them, Josef. It was their fault.
They misled you like they've misled everybody.

STALIN: And I was enjoying it so much. Did you enjoy it,
Prokofiev?

PROKOFIEV: Yes. And I'm sorry that it failed but at least we all
had the wit to realize it. After all, we can always try again.

STALIN: You'd do that with a good heart?

PROKOFIEV: Definitely.

STALIN: Shostakovich?

SHOSTAKOVICH: More time would help. You can't rush these
things.

STALIN: I don't think you enjoyed it much. You don't enjoy
anything, do you? Tell me, misery-guts, do you enjoy being
alive?

SHOSTAKOVICH: Not always.

STALIN: Do you know, it's very odd, but whenever I make a
mistake I go back in my mind to the days when I wanted to
be a priest. I was always in trouble, always, but all I
wanted in the whole world was to be the good shepherd in
the valley of the shadow of death. Thy rod. Thy staff. Me
comfort still. Fancy thinking that I was not cut out for it.
(STALIN *shakes his head and looks at his hands. He sings softly:*)
     He who clothes himself with light
     as with a garment,
       stood naked at the judgement . . .
(*He falls into a catatonic reverie, his eyes open. He hums a few more
bars then falls silent. Pause.* ZHDANOV *has a good look at him.*)

ZHDANOV: Josef!
(*Pause.* ZHDANOV *passes a hand in front of* STALIN*'s face. He does
not respond.*)
Josef!

STALIN: Josef Vissarion Djugashvili is my name. I want to be a
priest and save people. Have you any room for me?

ZHDANOV: Josef! Can you hear me? Do you want to go to bed?

STALIN: Josef Vissarion Djugashvili. The shoemaker's apprentice. God's apprentice. He's dead, you know. Further and further away from myself.

(ZHDANOV *snaps his fingers in front of* STALIN'*s eyes.* STALIN *laughs softly to himself, then suddenly grabs* ZHDANOV'*s hand. He holds it and forces* ZHDANOV *down.*)

If you come in on me from the right side you get my good arm, Comrade.

ZHDANOV: (*Prising his fist loose*) You're all right, Josef.

STALIN: Yes. I'm all right.

ZHDANOV: Good. (*Prises his hand out of* STALIN'*s fist.*) We still have these monkeys with us. Shall I get rid of them?

STALIN: They don't understand. But I want them. They're mine.

ZHDANOV: (*Standing up*) This man saved your country in its hour of peril. You are privileged to be near him. He won a great war.

STALIN: No one can take that away from me.

ZHDANOV: God help anyone that tries.

STALIN: God help anyone that tries.

(STALIN *suddenly gets to his feet and, very briskly, goes to the piano and pours himself a drink. He is full of energy again, back in command.*)

We'll have another go at it. But, I have to be frank with you, you made me suffer. I don't want to go through that again. All right, there're no guarantees, I know that, but we have to do a lot better this time. Well, say something! Come on! Andrei, I warn you, I'm starting to feel very hostile towards these two nincompoops. They're starting to get on my nerves.

ZHDANOV: That's the brightest thing you've said all night.

(STALIN *throws his vodka full in* ZHDANOV'*s face.* ZHDANOV *stands very still.* STALIN *pours another glass of vodka and walks towards* SHOSTAKOVICH *who sees what's coming and takes his glasses off.* STALIN *throws vodka in his face. He returns to the piano, fills another glass, goes to* PROKOFIEV, *dips his fingers in the vodka and sketches a cross on* PROKOFIEV'*s forehead.*)

In the name of Father, Son and Holy Ghost, amen. All is

forgiven. We're back where we started from. But this time we've got to do better . . . or else!

SHOSTAKOVICH: Are we going to try and salvage anything from the first effort . . .

STALIN: That abortion is finished with. It never existed. We never did it. It never happened. Not that. Not us. A new sound has to come out of somewhere.

SHOSTAKOVICH: Then we must have a new story. It's essential!

STALIN: I could kick you for that. It wasn't the story that was wrong. See, you're trying to fix the blame on me. It was the music that didn't work. When I think of my poor father. A family of serfs we came from. Serfs. (*Weeps.*) I'm off again. My mother was a saint. What she put with. (*Takes a drink.*) I was a great trial to her, you know. She knew about Tariel. She told me those tales in her own words. (*Pause.*) I feel as though I've let her down. Something's gone wrong.

ZHDANOV: Josef, with respect, I think we'll have to rejig that old tale. It's marvellous, of course, but a bit antiquated. What's the relevance of Tariel and his queer battle with these animals—aren't lions and tigers extinct here now?—to the Soviet Union today, as it stands? Not only that but this is an élitist piece, drawn from one region, a region that is more fortunate than a place like, well, Siberia. At least let's move this knight to Siberia and let him run into a bear and a wolf.

STALIN: A wolf? Now you're talking!

ZHDANOV: Tariel comes face to face with real life, the truth, call it what you like. Don't you think that's a much better idea? And, while we're at it, do we actually need any reptiles around?

STALIN: I like wolves. Seven years of my life spent exiled in Siberia brought them very close. I used to watch the wolves running over the snowfields—dogs mating with bitches, cubs learning to hunt, scarred old loners hanging around on the edges of the pack, sick ones being picked off, old ones fading. Those animals kept me warm, reminded of life. Yes, I'd like to go back to Siberia on a sentimental journey. It was my second home.

65

ZHDANOV: Pack your kit! We're moving out!

SHOSTAKOVICH: I don't like the cold.

STALIN: Things are clearer in the cold. You see the world as it is: cruel, murderous, hostile. But the cold provokes life. All the energy has to come from within. The cold is creative. The true, true sun is inside oneself.

SHOSTAKOVICH: Inside one oneself. You.

STALIN: You can't take the cold, my son? How is it that Russia is your home? What go ye into the desert to find? A man in soft raiment? Yes, it's the sun inside me that keeps the land warm at all! Do you know why Julius Caesar would not accept a crown? It was less than he had already.

PROKOFIEV: Is that our insurance against the restoration of the Tsar?

(ZHDANOV *laughs*.)

STALIN: I'm glad you're feeling easier with me. There is no insurance any more. We nationalized it. (*Roars with laughter*.) I am the past, Prokofiev; I make the present; and I will supervise the future. No wonder you feel more relaxed. (*Pause*.) Why haven't you two set any work by Jack London to music? He's the best writer the West has ever produced. And a red-hot socialist into the bargain.

PROKOFIEV: Oh, you like him, do you? Doesn't he spend rather a lot of time in the minds of animals?

STALIN: Yes. What's the matter with that? Look at yourself? You're dying. Look at Andrei? He's on his way out. It's the animal part that has the real power. Find the secret of that and you've solved everything. Jack London. Wonderful writer. Probably a Slav in his family somewhere, eh? Beneath it all, all the talk, all the organization, we are animals. *The Call of the Wild*. 'The Indians tell of a Ghost Dog that runs at the head of the pack. They are afraid of this Ghost Dog for it has cunning greater than they, stealing from their camps in fierce winters, robbing their traps, slaying their dogs, and defying their hunters.' Catch the mood, Prokofiev! Catch the mood!

PROKOFIEV: I'm not much of a one for the great outdoors.

STALIN: Hothouse plant! Orchid! How dare you write about

wolves! What d'you know about them? You've been misleading millions of children with that *Peter and the Wolf* thing of yours. They'll think that wolves are there to be played with.

PROKOFIEV: I don't know. My wolf is savage enough. (*Plays the Wolf theme from* Peter and the Wolf.) He eats people. I'd say he was a very naughty wolf indeed.

STALIN: Where's his strength? Where's his power? The wolf is always with us, waiting to burst out. 'When the long winter nights come on and the wolves follow their meat into the lower valleys, the Ghost Dog may be seen running at the head of the pack through the pale moonlight or glimmering borealis, leaping gigantic above his fellows, his great throat a-bellow as he sings a song of the younger world, which is the song of the pack.'

(*Pause.* PROKOFIEV *lightly plays the Wolf theme again in a jocular way.*)

You're a thousand miles away with that. No wonder you can't get through to ordinary people. They know what the power of Nature is. They feel it.

(*He goes to a huge wall mirror.*)

PROKOFIEV: Do you worship Nature?

STALIN: I was taught to worship God. They were hard men who taught me. They used force. We can all become God if we grind away at it. That's Christian teaching.

(*He stares into the mirror.*)

PROKOFIEV: And the wolf? Can he become God?

STALIN: The animal is always holy. That was the first work of God, the beasts. Grrrr! Bahooo! White Fang! Red claw! Grrrroah!

PROKOFIEV: Tariel, the oversexed Georgian outmoded militarist, a man in the peak of condition, climbs a sharp gradient (*Improvises.*) encounters a lion and tiger in the act of bestial coition and Jack London with an enormous wolf on a lead. Tariel is not confused. Being an educated man his mind turns to thinking how to exploit this galaxy of sexual opportunities. But what's this? The lion, the tiger and the wolf have set up a ménage à trois and are tearing the seats

67

out of Tariel's and Jack London's trousers. 'My God,'
the humans cry and run home to their respective mothers.
Meanwhile, back in the Kremlin, Ivan the Terrible is
growing hair all over his body . . . there's a full moon . . .
madness . . .

(*Pause. They look at* STALIN *who is grimly silent. Then* ZHDANOV
suddenly roars with laughter. STALIN *leaves the piano and goes over
to* ZHDANOV. *For a moment it looks as though he might hit him but
he merely slides his arm round* ZHDANOV's *shoulder then steals his
drink. They sport like a couple of boys.*)

ZHDANOV: Get your own!

STALIN: Come on, meanie!

ZHDANOV: Get off me! I want my idea discussed seriously. I'm
the one who has to go back and chair that bloody
conference tomorrow and I must have something to tell
them, be able to show we've made some progress, taken a
few decisions. Let's move the whole thing to Siberia.

STALIN: Too crowded.

ZHDANOV: Too crowded!

(*They roar with laughter, holding on to each other.* PROKOFIEV *nods
and smiles, playing gentle music on the piano.* SHOSTAKOVICH *sings
quietly.* STALIN *balances a glass of vodka on his forehead, gyrating
slowly.*)

SHOSTAKOVICH: My woeful heart is a caravanserai, serai, serai,
serai.

ZHDANOV: All those who want this arsehole of a poncy, cock-
eyed, idiot knight transferred to the bloody tundra say aye!
(*Pause.*) Aye!

PROKOFIEV: I'm easy.

SHOSTAKOVICH: Me too. You can send him to anywhere you like
as far as I'm concerned. It's the story that matters. It's
man against Nature. That's the theme. It's very sad.

STALIN: You always did write miserable music.

SHOSTAKOVICH: Did I?

STALIN: What have you got to be miserable about?

SHOSTAKOVICH: It just seems to turn out that way.

STALIN: Answer the question. Why do you write such miserable,
whining, complaining dirges all the time?

(*Pause.* ZHDANOV *disentangles himself from* STALIN.)

SHOSTAKOVICH: I write from what I feel. Maybe I'm a
depressive.

STALIN: You abuse your status. People look up to you. And what
do you do for them? You unload your own self-indulgent
misery on them. You make them unhappy. That can't be
justified.

PROKOFIEV: Perhaps it is melancholy rather than misery?

ZHDANOV: Don't split hairs, you fucking dilettante! Here he is,
living in the most stirring times Russia has ever seen, and
all he does is make people want to commit suicide. What
right has he got to do that? Why don't you cheer the
buggers up for a change?

STALIN: I know why he does it. He's disappointed with the way
things have gone. He hates the Government. He feels out of
place.

SHOSTAKOVICH: That's not so . . .

STALIN: Yes it is! You're undermining us! Sit down. Play us
some of your miserable, horrible music so we can all have a
good cry. Go on. I'm in the mood for it.

(SHOSTAKOVICH *sits down at the piano.* PROKOFIEV *gives him a
pat on the shoulder and moves away.*)

Come on, make us miserable. We all want to die. Russia is
a failure. The great experiment has been a disaster. All
happiness has been destroyed.

SHOSTAKOVICH: I don't believe that.

ZHDANOV: Play or I'll smash your head in! My life's work being
pissed on by a neurotic nancy-boy like you! Go on, tell me.
Make me cry.

(SHOSTAKOVICH *starts to play a piano theme from the Trio No. 2,
Op. 67. At first he falters but he becomes involved with the music and
strengthens his playing.*)

Boo hoo! Everything's a mess.

STALIN: Shut up, you ignorant pig! (*Pause.*) Who is this music
for, Shostakovich?

SHOSTAKOVICH: For the dead.

(*He plays on.* STALIN *drinks more. He leans against the
mantelshelf.*)

STALIN: Do you know how many died? I hardly dare think of the number. I could not bear to see it written down. Should I whisper it to you?

(SHOSTAKOVICH *plays on, shaking his head.*)

Twenty million. Don't tell anyone, will you? Twenty million.

> My heart is a caravanserai.
> To him who has been struck in the liver
> by a snake treacle is better suited
> than red candy. To him who is dying of poison
> antidote is everything.
> Twenty million.
> An entire generation.

(SHOSTAKOVICH *stops playing.* STALIN *goes over to him and takes his hand. He kisses it.*)

Do you know why your music isn't liked any more?

SHOSTAKOVICH: No, no.

STALIN: Remember before the war how they all loved you?

SHOSTAKOVICH: Yes, I do.

STALIN: You have lost that audience. Not your fault. They were the ones who died in the war, the twenty million.

SHOSTAKOVICH: I know, I know.

(SHOSTAKOVICH *lowers his head.*)

STALIN: Now there are only old folk and children. All the life has to come from me. (*Pause.*) You must stop mourning for the dead. Give the old folk and children what they need to cheer them up. They have to work hard these days.

(SHOSTAKOVICH *lowers his head until it touches the keyboard.*)

The old folk prefer old music. The children learn from the grandparents because their fathers and mothers are dead. So, it is old music we need—Tchaikovsky, I'm afraid, Rimsky, all the old favourites. Do it for me.

(SHOSTAKOVICH *bangs his head on the keyboard, crying.* STALIN *sits next to him and plays the theme from the* Pathétique. PROKOFIEV *pours himself a drink and tosses it back, hurling the glass into the fireplace.* ZHDANOV *laughs curtly, pours himself a glass of vodka, drinks it, then pours another and drinks it, then hurls his glass into the fireplace.*)

SHOSTAKOVICH: All I can hear is their silence. I don't know what they are saying. It's all been washed away.

ZHDANOV: They're saying get on with it!

STALIN: Prokofiev, you must face it as well. Your greatest fans are in the graveyard.

PROKOFIEV: I'll be joining them before long.

STALIN: Don't keep writing for them. You can compose like anyone you want. If I told you to imitate Beethoven, you could do it, and better the original.

PROKOFIEV: Could I? Beethoven was a German. I don't feel like writing like a German. Is that surprising?

STALIN: You know what I mean.

PROKOFIEV: We are already servants of one compulsion—our work. What you are asking would put us into a double servitude. Why not take what is Caesar's and leave us something to write with—a small freedom which is, after all, something of a secret.

STALIN: I don't like secrets. You'll do as you're told.

PROKOFIEV: You're expecting too much of us.

STALIN: Why? All I'm asking you to do is go back to being a student again. It's never too late to learn.

ZHDANOV: Do it for the cripples running the factories, the children in the fields twelve hours a day. Make sense of their drudgery. It will take fifty years for us to recover from the war. Extend our traditions of music to cover that period and Russia will be grateful.

STALIN: Exactly, Andrei, exactly. Well done. That's put it in a nutshell. They can do it. They're geniuses, these two. If you're a genius in the Soviet Union today you have terrible responsibilities—as I know, to my cost. (*Pause.*) All those unfulfilled lives wasted in war are my destiny. I must live them out. I'll survive to be a thousand, a thousand thousand. In the stalks of young gooseberries is a substance that prolongs life. Georgian gooseberries, of course. (*Pause.*)

ZHDANOV: So, you two know what you must do.

STALIN: They're good men. I trust them.

ZHDANOV: We'll go back to the conference and sort this out. I'm not going to stand up there and say—everyone has to write old music.

STALIN: Tsarist, bourgeois, capitalist music. Get it right. (*Picks up the icon.*) Old friends are best. Old enemies are better.

ZHDANOV: I'm not going to say that. I'll find a way of putting it over. But I need your help with the decree. Am I going to get it?

(*Pause.* STALIN *sits down, holding the icon to his chest.*)

PROKOFIEV: We will do what we can, within reason. Our kind of reason.

ZHDANOV: That's not enough . . .

STALIN: That is enough. They're going to write music like Tchaikovsky from now on. I know them. They're good Russians. They'll sacrifice their individuality like I have. Who am I now? I don't exist any more as a man. Stalin died in the war. Two lives I've lost. God lives in light, alone.

(STALIN *falls asleep. Pause.* ZHDANOV *looks at him, turns and looks at the composers, putting his finger to his lips. He takes off his jacket and covers* STALIN *up with it. Pause. He holds out his hand for* PROKOFIEV'*s and* SHOSTAKOVICH'*s jackets. They take them and hand them over.* ZHDANOV *covers* STALIN *with them, then beckons the others to leave. They wait for him by the door.* ZHDANOV *turns out the light.*)

PROKOFIEV: Please pass on our thanks to Comrade Stalin for a most instructive and helpful evening.

ZHDANOV: See you at the conference tomorrow. Good night.

PROKOFIEV: Good night.

SHOSTAKOVICH: Good night.

(ZHDANOV *ushers them out, then exits himself, closing the door behind him.* STALIN *sleeps on in the darkness. Bix Beiderbecke plays 'Old Man River' on his cornet again as total blackout closes in.*)